"Before you go, there's something I just have to do," Austin said.

She released a weary sigh. "What now?"

"This."

He framed her face in his palms and covered her mouth with his before she had time to issue a protest. She knew she should pull away, but as it had always been, she was completely captive to the softness of his lips, the gentle stroke of his tongue, his absolute skill. No one had ever measured up to him when it came to kissing. She suspected no one ever would.

Once they parted, Austin tipped his forehead against hers. "Man, I've missed this."

"We're not children anymore, Austin. We can't go back to the way it was."

He took an abrupt step back. "I'm not suggesting we do that. But we can go forward, see where it goes."

"It won't go anywhere because you'll never be able to give me what I want."

"What do you want, Georgie?"

"More."

* * *

An Heir for the Texan is part of the Texas Extreme series—Six rich and sexy cowboy brothers live—and love—to the extreme!

Dear Reader,

After writing forty-plus books, I've found it challenging at times to come up with creative names for characters. However, it's even harder to when it comes to livestock and pets. Of course, if you're composing a book set on a ranch, chances are you're going to have various animals. Sometimes a lot of animals.

This story happens to feature several horses and, frankly, I dreaded naming them. Then suddenly I had an epiphany (duh moment)—I used to own a horse ranch, and every horse had a nickname. So there you go. Each majestic beast featured in this book carries the moniker of a horse I once owned. Bubba, although portrayed as a gelding, was a two-time national champion Appaloosa stallion and the father of several offspring before his untimely death at five. Junior was the first horse I rode competitively, and Butterball was my daughter's Shetland pony, just to name a few. All held a special place in our family, and our hearts, and I've included them as a tribute to all the joy they brought to our lives.

As far as the humans go, I hope you enjoy Austin Calloway's journey into the past that leads to a promising future, despite all the ups and downs he encounters when reuniting with his very first love, Georgie Romero, although he doesn't dare admit that. If luck prevails, perhaps Georgie will be his last...

Happy reading!

Kristi

KRISTI GOLD

—

AN HEIR FOR THE TEXAN

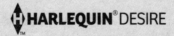

Recycling programs
for this product may
not exist in your area.

ISBN-13: 978-0-373-83821-9

An Heir for the Texan

Printed in U.S.A.

www.Harlequin.com

Kristi Gold has a fondness for beaches, baseball and bridal reality shows. She firmly believes that love has remarkable healing powers, and she feels very fortunate to be able to weave stories of love and commitment. As a bestselling author, a National Readers' Choice Award winner and a three-time Romance Writers of America RITA® Award finalist, Kristi has learned that although accolades are wonderful, the most cherished rewards come from networking with readers. She can be reached through her website at kristigold.com, or through Facebook.

Books by Kristi Gold

Harlequin Desire

Visit her Author Profile page at Harlequin.com, or kristigold.com, for more titles.

To my former farrier and dear friend Stephanie S., and her fantastic mother-in-law, Florence, for all the support they've shown me throughout the years.

Love ya both.

One

If Austin Calloway had to hang one more damn holiday light, he'd book a flight to the Bahamas to ring in the New Year.

For the past six Decembers, the D Bar C Ranch—his home, both past and present—had morphed from a South Texas ranch into a fake winter wonderland, all in the name of community involvement. Next week, the chaos would begin with cars lining up to bask in the holiday glow and deliver toys for underprivileged children. As much as he appreciated the cause, he didn't particularly care for the effort involved in transforming the place, especially while being supervised by two nitpicky female relatives.

After draping the last string on the barbed wire, Austin hopped off the fence flanking the entry and climbed onto the ATV, taking off through the main gate toward temporary freedom. He passed by the family homestead, where his sister-in-law, Paris, sat on the front porch, hands resting on her pregnant belly. He raised his hand in a wave, and grinned when he noticed his brother, Dallas, struggling to set up the inflatable Santa beneath the massive oak while his blond-haired bride cheered him on. But his smile faded fast when he thought about his own failed marriage, and the loneliness that plagued him during the holidays.

Shaking off the self-pity, Austin picked up speed before someone chased him down, namely one of the two self-proclaimed elves now hanging angels on the manicured hedges. As much as he appreciated Maria, the former nanny who'd become his much loved stepmom after the death of his birth mother, and Jenny, the surprise stepmom they'd only learned about six years ago during the reading of his father's will, he was more than done with the decorating demands.

Once he rounded the corner and reached his own cedar-and-rock house, he pulled into the driveway, shut down the ATV, then slid into the cab of his dual-wheel truck. He backed out and retraced the path he had taken, not bothering to acknowledge the family members standing on the lawn, shooting dagger looks in his direction. He continued toward the safety of the highway as he headed to an atmosphere where he could feel more macho.

A few miles down the road, Austin pulled into the gravel parking lot at the outdoor arena and claimed a spot among all the stock trailers, plagued by past memories of the life he'd left behind. He'd said good-bye to the rodeo circuit several years ago to enter the cutthroat world of car dealerships. Actually, several truck dealerships spanning three states, thanks to the help of his winnings and inheritance. At least he'd succeeded at that endeavor, even if he had failed at his marriage.

Shaking off the regrets, he walked through the entry, nodding at several cowboys, some who had been his competition. He immediately noticed all the young bucks crowded round the catch pens, eyeing him with awe like he was some sort of rodeo god. Those glory days were long gone and only remnants of the memories remained. But at least he'd left some sort of positive legacy to some kids since he'd probably never have any of his own.

He climbed the steps two at a time and slid onto a wooden bench as a spectator, not a participant. That's when he spotted her rounding the arena—a great-looking filly he knew all too well. A literal blast from his past. She was as flighty as a springtime moth, and as stubborn as a rusty gate. She could bring a man down with the swish of her tail. Austin should know. She'd brought him to his knees on more than one occasion. And even though several years had passed since he'd last seen her, he fondly recalled how she'd always given him a damn good ride.

He shifted slightly as he watched her weave in and out of traffic, black mane flowing behind her in the breeze. She hadn't lost her spirit, or her skill, or her ability to completely captivate him.

Austin tensed when he noticed a gelding coming toward her, trying his best to buck off the cowboy on his back. If the filly didn't slow down, move over, an equine wreck was imminent.

No sooner than he'd thought it, it happened. The filly in question went one way, the mare she was riding went the other, and Georgie Romero, his black-maned, flighty, spirited first real girlfriend, ended up on the ground in a heap.

A distant memory from his early childhood shot through Austin's mind in response. The recollection of his own mother falling from her horse when he'd been too young to comprehend the consequences, or the impending loss. When he'd been too little to understand.

That alone sent him on a sprint toward the arena in an effort to come to *this* woman's rescue. He damn sure didn't want to relive that tragedy.

He hoped like hell this time he wasn't too late.

When Georgia May Romero opened her eyes, she sensed a gathering crowd, but a pair of brown boots earned her immediate focus. She then noticed jean-encased legs and two large masculine hands resting casually on bent knees. And next—one very impressive, extremely big…belt buckle.

Clearly she had died and gone to Cowboy Heaven.

Her gaze traveled upward to take in the blue plaid shirt rolled up at the sleeves, revealing arms threaded with masculine veins and, above that, an open collar showing a slight hint of chest hair. She then visually journeyed to a whisker-shaded jaw surrounding a stellar mouth and an average nose with a slight indentation on the bridge. But there was nothing average about the midnight blue eyes. Devilish eyes. Familiar eyes. Surely not.

"You okay, Georgie?"

No, she'd died and gone to Cowgirl Hell.

Shaking off her stupor, Georgie sat up and scrambled to her feet, silently cursing her bad luck and the man standing before her. The only man who could shake her to the core with only a smile. The man who'd changed her life six years ago, and he didn't even know it. "Where's my horse?"

He pointed toward the outside of the arena. "Over there, tied to the rail. She's a little bit shaken but she's physically fine."

Only then did she venture another glance at her walking past, Austin Calloway. "Thanks," she muttered. "She's a two-year-old and still a little green. I brought her out to get used to the crowds. Obviously she's not ready for competition."

He had the gall to grin. "I figured that much when she tossed you on your head. You fell pretty hard."

Oh, but she had…for him. Ancient history, one she didn't dare repeat despite this chance meeting.

Chance.

She did a frantic search for the dark-haired, hazel-eyed boy who'd been the love of her life for the past five years, and thankfully spotted him still seated in the stands, holding cowboy court with a host of familiar men laughing at his antics. Andy Acosta, the middle-aged father of five, and horse trainer extraordinaire, sat at Chance's side. Not only had Andy been a longtime hand on her family's ranch, he happened to be one of the few people she trusted with her son.

"Are you sure you're okay, Georgie? No headache or double vision? Broken bones?"

Just a pain in her keister. "I'm fine," she said as she tore her gaze from her son to Austin and tried to appear calm. Having him learn of her own child's existence, and the risk of prodding questions, was the last thing she needed at the moment. When she'd made the decision to move back to town to establish her veterinarian practice, she'd known she would have to tell him eventually, but she wanted to prolong that revelation until she'd had more time to prepare. Until she could gauge how he might react. Standing in a busy arena wasn't an appropriate venue to deliver that bombshell.

"You don't look fine," he said. "In fact, you look a little out of it."

She swept the dirt from her butt with her palms and frowned. "I assure you I'm okay. It's not the first time I've been bucked off."

He took off his tan felt hat, forked a hand through his golden brown hair, then set it back on his head. "True. I remember that summer you broke your arm when you tried to ride your dad's stallion."

Leave it to him to bring that up. "I remember when you broke your nose getting into a fight with Ralphie Jones over Hannah Alvarez."

He smiled again, throwing her for a mental loop. "Hey, he started it. Besides, I didn't really like her all that much, and I was young and pretty stupid."

She'd been the same way at that time, and the price for her naivety had been high—losing her virginity to him. "Look, it's been nice seeing you again, but I have to go."

He inclined his head and frowned. "How long are you going to be in town?"

She considered lying but realized he would eventually learn the truth. At least one truth. "Indefinitely."

He looked shocked, to say the least. "You're living here now?"

"Yes."

"How long have you been back?"

She wasn't in the mood for a barrage of questions, although she did have one of her own. "A couple of weeks. Dallas didn't tell you?"

He scowled. "No. Dallas doesn't tell me a damn thing. When did you see him?"

"Actually, he called me after he learned I've taken over Doc Gordon's practice. He asked me if I'd be the vet for the D Bar C, and this new venture you have in the works, although he didn't exactly explain what that entails other than it involves livestock."

"We're calling it Texas Extreme," he said. "We're starting a business that caters to people who want the whole cowboy experience. Roping and bull riding and all things rodeo, plus we're considering a good old-fashioned trail ride."

Just what the Calloways needed—another business that would pad their pockets even more. "Interesting. I don't think the ranch house is large enough to accommodate guests and your brothers, so I assume you're going to put them in the bunkhouse."

"We're in the process of building a lodge. And since you've been away awhile, you probably don't know that we've all built our own houses. Or at least Dallas, Houston, Tyler, Worth and me. Fort won't step foot on the place. He basically hates the entire family."

She recalled how upset Austin had been when he'd learned he had twin brothers, Forth and Worth, and a stepmother in Louisiana, thanks to a bigamist father who'd revealed all after his death. She also remembered how Austin had turned to her following the reading of the will, and his distress that had led to her providing comfort. If only she could forget that night, but she'd been left with a constant, precious reminder.

Georgie sent a sideways glance toward her son, who fortunately didn't seem interested in her whereabouts. But if she didn't get away soon, he might notice her and flag her down. Worse still, call her "Mama." Then she'd have to explain everything. Almost everything. She backed up a couple of steps and hooked a thumb over her shoulder. "I guess I better go now."

"You aren't competing in the barrel racing with a more seasoned horse?" he asked.

She shook her head. "Not today."

He favored her with another sexy grin. "Guess I'll be heading out, too."

"But you just got here." And she'd just given herself away.

His smile faded into a confused look. "How do you know that?"

She studied the dirt at her feet before raising her gaze to his. "I saw you take a seat in the stands." The distraction had resulted in her lack of concentration in the arena, and the fact that he'd come to her rescue still stunned her.

He hooked both thumbs in his pockets, causing her to glimpse a place no self-respecting mother should notice, and it wasn't his buckle. "I was only here to escape all the holiday decorating at the ranch," he said. "If I don't get back, my stepmom is bound to send out a posse."

She forced herself to look at his face. "How is Maria?"

"Feisty as ever. How are your folks?"

Georgie didn't care to broach that topic in detail, and preferred to let Austin assume she still lived at home. That would guarantee he wouldn't come calling, considering the long-standing feud between both their families, compliments of their competitive fathers. Only one time had a Calloway son entered their abode. Through her bedroom window. She had given Austin everything that night eighteen years ago, including her heart. "Mom and Papa are doing fine," she said, banishing the bittersweet memories from her mind.

"I'm sure they're glad to have you back from school. I bet Old George is strutting around like a rooster over his only kid becoming a veterinarian."

Not so much. Her father was still shamed over having a daughter who'd had a baby out of wedlock, information her family had kept away from the public eye. In fact, she hadn't spoken to her dad to any degree in years. Luckily her mother hadn't passed judgment and still supported her when she'd stayed away from the small town and the prospect of gossip. She purposefully lost touch with friends, and now that she'd returned, she'd fortunately been able to find a remote place of her own, even if it was only a rental. But eventually everyone would know about her son because she couldn't hide out forever, nor did she want to.

When Chance waved, Georgie tried for a third departure. "Well, I better load up and leave before the competition begins."

A slight span of silence passed before Austin spoke again. "You look real good, Georgie girl."

So did he. Too good. Otherwise she might scold him for calling her by his pet name. "Thanks. I'll see you around."

"You most definitely will."

Georgie disregarded the comment, turned away and then walked through the gate to retrieve her mare. She lingered there for a few moments and watched Austin leave the arena before seeking out her son. "Let's go, Chance," she called as she untied the horse and started down the aisle.

Chance scampered down from the bleachers and came to her side, his face and baseball cap smeared with dirt. "Who was that man, Mama?"

Oh, heavens. She had so hoped he hadn't noticed. "Austin Calloway."

"Who is he?"

She kept right on walking as she considered how

she should answer. She settled on a partial truth instead of full disclosure as she walked toward her trailer, her baby boy at her side.

"He's an old friend, sweetie."

An old friend who'd been her first lover. Her first love. Her one and only heartbreak. But most important, the father of her child.

If or when Austin Calloway learned that she'd been withholding that secret, she could only imagine how he would react—and it wouldn't be good.

Austin stormed into the main house to seek out the source of his anger. He found him in the parlor where they'd grown up, his pregnant wife seated in his lap. "I've got a bone to pick with you, Dallas."

Both Dallas and Paris stared at him like he'd grown a third eye, then exchanged a look. "I think I'll go see if Maria and Jenny need help with dinner," Paris said as she came to her feet.

Dallas patted her bottom. "Good idea. I can't feel my legs."

She frowned and pointed down at her belly. "Hush. This is all your fault, so complaining is not allowed."

"You sure didn't complain when I got you that way," Dallas added with a grin as his wife headed toward the kitchen.

Watching his brother and sister-in-law's banter

didn't sit well with Austin. "If you're done mooning over your bride, we need to talk."

Dallas leaned back on the blue floral sofa that Jenny had brought with her, draped an arm over the back and crossed his boots at his ankles. "Have a seat and say what's on your mind."

Austin eyed the brown leather chair but decided he was too restless to claim it. "I don't want to have a seat."

"Then stand, dammit. Just get on with it."

He remained planted in the same spot even though he wanted to pace. "Why the hell didn't you tell me Georgia Romero was back in town?"

"Georgia's back in town?" came from the opening to his right.

Austin turned his attention to Maria, his stepmother, mentor and crusader for the truth, and sometimes intruder into conversations. "So he didn't tell you, either?"

Dallas's jaw tightened and his eyes narrowed. "I'd forgotten I'd talked to her day before yesterday. Besides, it's not that big a deal. A drought is a big deal."

"It's a big deal to your little brother, *mijo*," Maria said as she tightened the band at the end of her long braid. "Austin and Georgia have a special relationship."

Obviously the family was intent on throwing the past up in his face like prairie dirt. "*Had* a relationship. That was a long time ago."

Dallas smirked. "You'd take her back as your girl-friend in a New York minute."

"You have a girlfriend, sugar?"

Enter the blonde, bouncy second stepmom. The woman Austin's dad had married without divorcing Maria. Jenny was a good-hearted gossip and that alone made him want to walk right back out the door. Doing so would only prolong the conversation, un-fortunately. "No, Jen, I don't have a girlfriend."

"He used to have a girlfriend," Maria added. "Georgia and Austin were real close in high school."

Jenny laid a dramatic palm on her chest below the string of pearls. "I just love Georgia. Atlanta in the springtime is…"

"Focus, woman," Maria scolded. "We're talkin' about a girl, not a state."

Jenny lifted her chin. "I know that, Maria. You're telling me about Austin being joined at the hip to his high school sweetheart, who happens to be named Georgia."

Dallas chuckled. "You've got that 'joined at the hip' thing right, Jen, but Austin chased her for years before that *joining*."

Austin needed to set this part of the record straight. "I damn sure didn't chase her." Much. "She hung around all of us when we were kids. I never paid her any mind back then."

"Not until she came back from camp that summer after she turned fourteen," Dallas said.

Man, he hadn't thought about that in years. She'd returned with a lot of curves that would make many a hormone-ridden guy stand up and take notice. Every part of him. She still had a body that wouldn't quit, something he'd noticed earlier. Something he wouldn't soon forget. "Yep, she'd definitely blossomed that summer."

"You mean she got her boobies," Jenny chimed in. "Mine came in at twelve. That's when the boys started chasing me like Louisiana mosquitoes."

Maria waved a dismissive hand at Jen. "No one wants to know when you reached puberty and how many times you got a love bite."

Austin didn't want to continue this bizarre conversation. Luckily Paris showed up to end the weird exchange. "Dinner will be ready in about five minutes."

Jenny turned her attention to Austin. "Maybe you should invite your special friend to dinner."

Of all of the stupid ideas—subjecting Georgie to an ongoing conversation about puberty. Then again, he wouldn't mind sitting across a table from her. He wouldn't mind her sitting in his lap, either. "It's late and I'm sure she's busy."

Paris perked up like a hound coming upon a rabbit's scent. "She? So that's what you were discussing in my absence."

Dallas pushed off the sofa. "Yeah, and boobies and mosquitoes."

"Don't ask, Paris," Maria stated. "Now you boys wash up while we put the food on the table."

No way would he subject himself to more talk about his history with Georgie. "I'm not staying for dinner."

"Suit yourself," Dallas said. "But you'll be missing out on Jen's chicken-fried steak."

Any other time he would reconsider, but not today. "I'm sure it'll be great. Before I take off, Dallas, we need to finish our conversation."

His brother shrugged. "I'm listening."

When Austin noticed the women still hovering, he added, "In private. Outside."

Dallas sighed. "Fine. Just make it quick. I'm starving."

He had every intention of making it quick while getting his point across.

After they walked out the door onto the porch, Austin faced his brother. "Look, I would've appreciated you consulting all the brothers before you hired Georgie as the ranch vet."

Dallas streaked a hand over his jaw. "Actually, I did. Houston doesn't have a problem with it, and neither does Tyler. Worth doesn't know about it but he trusts my judgment, unlike you."

Austin's ire returned with the force of a tornado. "You consulted them but you didn't bother to ask me?"

"Majority rules, and I figured you weren't going

to be too keen on the idea after the way you two ended it."

"What the hell does it matter what happened when we were in high school?"

"I meant six years ago, after the reading of Dad's will."

"How did you know we hooked up then?"

"Georgie called me a few months later and asked how she could get in touch with you. By that time you'd already married Abby. When I told her about that, she was upset. In other words, you broke her heart. Again."

Yeah, he probably had, and he'd never been proud of it. "It was just one night, Dallas, and I didn't marry Abby until four months later, so I wasn't cheating on either Georgie or Abby. Besides, I married Abby on a whim."

"A whim involving a woman you barely knew."

Only a partial truth. "Not so. I'd known Abby for years. I just didn't date her on a regular basis."

"But you did date Georgie at one time, and she's not the kind of woman to take sex lightly."

He was inclined to agree but decided not to give Dallas the pleasure of knowing he was right. "Georgie and I agreed no promises, no expectations, the last time we were together."

"Maybe you didn't have any expectations, but I suspect she did. She's always loved you, brother. I wouldn't be surprised if she still did, although I don't get why she would after the way you've treated her."

He didn't welcome his brother's counsel or condemnation. "You're a fine one to talk, Dallas. You left a trail of broken hearts all over the country."

"Yeah, but it only took one woman to set me straight."

"A woman you married because you wanted to keep control of the ranch."

Dallas leaned against the porch railing. "In the beginning, that was true. But it didn't take me long to realize Paris could put an end to my wicked ways."

He'd thought that about Abby, too, but his ex-wife hadn't been as sure. In the end, they realized they'd had no choice but to go their separate ways after rushing into a marriage that should never have taken place. "I'm glad for your good fortune, Dallas. But I don't think that woman exists for me."

Dallas's expression turned suddenly serious. "If you open your eyes, you might just see you've already found her. In fact, you ran into her today."

With that, Dallas went back inside, leaving Austin to ponder his words. True, he'd always had a thing for Georgie, but he'd chalked that up to chemistry. And she'd always been a beautiful woman, even during her tomboy phase. But he couldn't see himself with her permanently. See himself with anyone for that matter.

He'd already wrecked one marriage and he wasn't going to wreck another. He refused to fail again.

That said, if he and Georgie decided to mutually enjoy each other's company down the road, he wouldn't hate it. As long as she understood that he wasn't in the market for a future.

When it came to Georgia May Romero—and his ever-present attraction to her—keeping his hands to himself would be easier said than done.

"How's your first day as the Calloway vet going, Georgie girl?"

Fine…until he'd walked into the main barn dressed in chambray and denim, looking like every gullible girl's dream. Yet when she decided to accept Dallas's job offer, she'd known seeing Austin would be a strong possibility. In fact, that had been part of her reasoning to sign on as the resident veterinarian—to size him up, but only when it came to his life, not his looks. However, she was still a bit shaken over their encounter yesterday, and she was bent on ignoring him today.

For that reason, and many more, she continued putting away her equipment in the duffel without looking at him. "I was just vaccinating the pregnant mares."

"At least we only have four this year, not ten like in years past."

"True." Georgie straightened and patted the bay's

muzzle protruding through the rail. "I remember when this one was born, and that had to be fifteen years ago. We're both getting on up there in age, aren't we, Rosie? They should really give you a break from the babies."

Georgie sensed Austin moving toward her before he said, "She keeps churning out prime cattle horses, but hopefully Dallas will decide to retire her from the breeding program after this year."

"Good, although I'm sure she'll have no trouble foaling this year. Dallas did ask me to be here when Sunny foals since she's a maiden mare. I told him I'd try, although horses have given birth without help for centuries. Of course, I expect to have to pull a few calves in the future."

When he didn't respond to her rambling, she faced him and met his grin. "Do you find some sort of warped humor in that?"

He braced his hand on the wooden frame and leaned into it, leaving little distance between them. "No. It's just strange to see you doing your animal doctor thing."

Boy, did he smell good, like manly soap, as if he'd just walked out of the shower. She imagined him in the shower…with her. Slick, wet bodies and roving hands and… Good grief. "Are you worried I'm not qualified?"

His come-hither expression melted into a frown. "I have no reason to believe you're not qualified since you went to the best vet college in the country. I guess I'm just used to you riding horses, not giving them shots. It's going to take a while to adjust to the new you."

"I'm the same old me, Austin." And that had never been more apparent than when she continued to react to him on a very carnal level. "Only now I have a career that I've talked about since we were climbing trees together."

He reached out and tucked one side of her hair behind her ear. "Do you remember that one time we were in the tree near the pond on your property? You were twelve at the time, I believe."

What girl didn't remember her first kiss, even if it had been innocent and brief? "If you're referring to that day when you tried to put me in a lip-lock, I definitely recall what happened next."

His grin returned. "You slugged me."

"I barely patted your cheek."

"I almost toppled out of the tree. You didn't know your own strength."

He hadn't known how much she had wanted him to kiss her, or how scared she had been to let him. "That kind of thing was not at the top of my to-do list at that time."

"Maybe, but I found out kissing had moved to number one on the list that summer after you came back from camp."

She felt her face flush. "I was fourteen and you were fifteen and a walking case of hormones."

He inched a little closer. "You had hormones, too. They were in high gear that first night we made out behind the gym after the football game."

She shivered over the recollection. "Big deal. So you managed to get to first base."

His blue eyes seemed to darken to a color this side of midnight. "Darlin', I got to second base."

"Your fumbling attempts weren't exactly newsworthy."

Oddly, he didn't seem at all offended. "Maybe I was a little green that first time, but I got better as time went on."

Her mind whirled back to that evening full of out-of-control chemistry. She didn't want to acknowledge how vulnerable she'd been that particular night, and many nights after that when they'd met in secret. How completely lost she had been for three whole years, and she hadn't been able to tell one solitary soul. "We were so reckless and stupid and darn lucky. If my father would have ever found out I was with a Calloway boy—"

"He would've shot first and asked questions later. He'd probably do that now."

Time to turn the subject in a different direction. "I'd hoped that after J.D. died, my father would've buried the hatchet and been more neighborly to you and the brothers."

"Ain't gonna happen," Austin said. "Last month he called the sheriff when one of our heifers ended up on his property. He blamed us for not maintaining the shared fence line when it's his responsibility, too."

"That doesn't surprise me."

"I'm surprised he approves of you working for the enemy."

"Actually, he doesn't know because I haven't told him." Just one more secret in her arsenal.

Austin pushed away from the wall, giving her a little more room to breathe. "That's probably wise. It's not fun to suffer the wrath of George Romero. But he's bound to find out eventually."

She shrugged. "Yes, but it really doesn't matter. I'm all grown up now and I make my own decisions, not him."

He winked. "Yep, you're all grown up for sure."

Her heart executed a little-pitter patter in her chest. "I need to get back to work now."

"Me, too. If I don't get busy soon, I'm going to suffer the wrath of Dallas."

If she didn't leave soon, she might be subjected to another journey into their shared past, including their sex life. *Former* sex life. "I've got a very busy day ahead of me, so I'll see you later."

He moved closer, as if he didn't want her to leave. "Then business is good?"

"So far." Yet she wouldn't be tending to livestock for the remaining hours. She would be sending her son off on a trip without her for the first time since his birth.

"I'm glad you've returned, Georgie," he said as he finally stepped back. "And by the way, if you're not busy this evening, Maria wants you to have dinner with us. All the usual suspects will be there. Have you met Worth or his mom, Jenny?"

"No. I haven't had the opportunity yet."

"All the more reason for you to come."

But being close to Austin was the best reason to decline. "I'm not sure I'll be finished with everything before dinnertime."

"We don't usually eat until around seven. If you decide to join us, and we really hope you will, just show up. We'll set a place for you."

If she agreed, she would have to spend even more time with him, all the while trying to conceal her true feelings. If she didn't, she would insult Maria. "I'll think about it."

He grinned, started away then said without turning around, "I'll see you tonight."

His confidence drove her crazy. *He* drove her crazy. But right then she had only one immediate concern... Her son's impending departure.

Two

Georgie climbed into her truck and headed home to face what would probably prove to be one of the most difficult times of her life. After she pulled into the drive and slid from the cab, Chance rushed out of the door and ran to her as fast as his little legs would let him. He wrapped his arms around her waist and stared up at her, his grin showing the space where he'd just lost his first tooth. "Mama, did you see the rolling house?"

Georgie glanced to her right to find the massive RV parked on the dirt road leading to the barn. "I see that, baby. It's huge."

Chance let her go and rocked back and forth on

his heels, as if he was too excited to stand still. "Aunt Debbie said I could ride up front with Uncle Ben and she could stay in the back and play cards with Grandma."

No doubt the wily pair would be engaging in poker. "That sounds like a plan. Are you packed?"

He nodded vigorously. "Uh-huh. I gotta get some toys." He grabbed her by the hand and jerked her forward with his usual exuberance. "Come on, Mama."

"All right, already. Just hold your horses."

Chance released his grasp on her and threw open the front screen door. Georgie followed him inside to find her mother's sister, Debbie, decked out in a blue floral sundress and an inordinate amount of jewelry, and her Uncle Ben wearing a yellow polo and white shorts that revealed his usual golf tan that ran from the top of his bald head to his beefy legs. Not exactly December attire, but luckily the region had yet to experience any significant cold weather. But that was all about to change in the next two days, according to the forecast.

"Georgia May!" Debbie said as she crossed the room and drew Georgie into a hug. "You are still as pretty as ever."

Georgie stepped back and smiled. "You look great, too, Aunt Debbie. I love the blond hair."

Debbie patted her neatly coifed bob. "Glad you like it. I just wish I could say the same for my husband. When I got it done, he didn't say a word. I don't think he's even noticed."

"I noticed, woman." Uncle Ben crossed the room, picked Georgie up off her feet, hugged her hard and then put her back down. "You're still no bigger than a peanut, Georgie. And don't listen to Deb. She knows I'm jealous because she still has all her hair."

"So how are you enjoying retirement?" Georgie asked.

"Love it," Ben said. "We just drove all the way from California."

Debbie smiled. "Los Angeles was so wonderful and warm, but the traffic was horrible."

Chance tugged on Georgie's hand to garner her attention. "Can we go now, Mama?"

Georgie swallowed around an annoying lump in her throat when she thought about watching him leave without her. "Don't you need to pick out some toys?"

"Oh, yeah."

"Don't bring too many things, Chance." Her directive was lost on her child as he sprinted out of the room.

"Your place is really precious, Georgie," Debbie said as she surveyed the area. "And it's been so well done."

Quite the change from when Georgie had first seen it—a basic two-bedroom, one-bath rental with outdated everything. But the appeal had been in the ten surrounding acres, complete privacy and the four-stall red barn. "You can thank Mom for the restoration. She had the hardwoods refinished, put new carpet in the bedrooms, remodeled the kitchen, including appliances, and redid the entire bathroom before I moved in. As much as I appreciated the effort, I do think it was overkill for a house I don't own."

Right on cue, Lila Romero breezed into the room, her silver hair pulled back in a low bun, her peach slacks and white blouse heralding her classic taste in clothing. "I couldn't let you live in squalor, dear daughter."

Leave it to Lila to overexaggerate. "It wasn't that bad, Mom."

"It wasn't that good, either." Lila turned to her sister and sighed. "Georgie is such a nervous Nellie, I'm surprised she's actually allowing my grandson to go with us to Florida."

Ben turned to Georgie. "He'll be fine, pumpkin. I used to fly big jets holding hundreds of passengers, so rest assured, I can handle a forty-five-foot motor home."

Georgie took some comfort in knowing her son would be on the ground in good hands, not in mid-air. "I trust you, Uncle Ben. I'm more worried that Chance will drive you insane with all his energy."

Aunt Debbie patted her cheek. "Honey, we have eight grandchildren. We're used to high energy. We'll be stopping along the way and—"

"If he acts up, we'll lock him in the toilet." Uncle Ben topped off the comment with a teasing grin.

Chance ran back into the room, his arms full of stuffed animals, miniature trucks and his special blue pillow. "I'm ready. Can we go now?"

Georgie fought back the surge of panic. "Can I at least have a hug, baby boy?"

As if she sensed her daughter's distress, Lila took the toys from her grandson's grasp. "I'll put these in the RV while you tell your mama goodbye."

In that moment, Georgie appreciated her mother more than she could express. "Thanks, Mom."

"You're welcome, honey. Take your time."

After her family filed out the exit, Georgie knelt down on Chance's level and brushed a dark lock from his forehead. "You'll be a good boy, right?"

"I'll be good. I'll brush my teeth and go to bed on time. And I'll mind Grandma."

"Are you going to miss me?"

He rolled his eyes. "Yeah, Mama."

She drew him into her arms. "I'm going to miss you something awful, too. I love you, sweetie."

"I love you, Mama."

Georgie held him tightly until he began to wriggle away. "I gotta go now, okay?" he said, his hazel eyes flashing with excitement.

"Okay." She kissed his cheek and straightened. "Eat some vegetables while you're gone."

He wrinkled his nose. "Do I hafta?"

"Just a little. That's better than nothing."

After taking him by the hand, Georgie led her son to the RV where she earned one more hug, one more kiss and an understanding smile from her aunt. Chance scurried up the stairs with Debbie following behind him, and once he had disappeared, Georgie turned to her mother. "You'll call me later, right?"

Lila raised her hand as if taking an oath. "I swear I will report back to you on a regular basis. And I also swear I will not sell my grandson for gas money."

Georgie felt a little foolish. "I'm sorry, Mom, but this is the first time we've been away from each other for any length of time. He'll be gone for two weeks."

"Two weeks' worth of amusement parks that he'll dearly love." She laid a palm on Georgie's cheek. "I know it's hard, honey, yet there comes a time when you have to let go a little. I learned that the hard way with you."

"I know, Mom. It's just so difficult."

"It is for both myself and your father, even if he doesn't show it."

"I wouldn't know since he's clearly still refusing to speak to me, much less see me or Chance."

"He'll come around, and that reminds me…" Her mother hesitated a moment, which gave Georgie pause. "Speaking of fathers and their children, have you given any more consideration to telling Chance's father about him?"

She'd been considering it nonstop. "I'm still on

the fence about that. The hows and the whens and whether or not it would serve any purpose at this point in time."

"Honey, it would serve a major purpose. It would give your son the opportunity to know his dad. They deserve to know each other."

With that, Lila climbed on board and closed the door without awaiting her daughter's response.

As Georgie watched the RV drive away in a cloud of dust, she felt more alone than she had since she'd realized she would be raising a child on her own.

She could stay at home this evening, missing her baby boy. Or she could go to the Calloways for dinner. Then again, that would mean facing Austin while reuniting with his family. Several years had passed since she had seen Maria and the boys, and the thought of eating a frozen dinner held little appeal.

Decision made. Wise or not, she would go.

"She's not coming." That reality had become apparent to Austin with every passing moment.

Dallas stopped rocking the back porch glider and shot him a hard look in response to the comment. "You don't know that, Austin. Dinner isn't even on the table yet."

Austin pushed off the wooden chair and stared out at the fence row lined with mesquites. "Georgie is never late. If she'd decided to be here, she would've already shown up."

"For a man who claimed five minutes ago, twice, that he didn't care if she stepped foot through the door, you sure seem concerned."

He spun on his brother and glared at him. "I just don't like people to go back on their word."

Dallas leaned forward and rested his arms on his knees. "So she told you she'd be here for sure?"

He had him there. "Maybe not in so many words, but she did seem open to the idea."

"That's a stretch from saying yes."

Austin muttered a few curses as he collapsed back into the chair. "Doesn't matter one way or the other. I was just being nice when I asked her."

"You were wishful thinking, Austin. You can pro-test all you want but you've always had a thing for her. You still do."

Time for a subject change. "Tyler mentioned that Fort called you earlier today. What did he want?"

Dallas sighed. "A part of the proceeds from Texas Extreme."

Austin couldn't believe his stepbrother's nerve. "He's never even stepped foot on this place. Why the hell does he think he's entitled to any profit aside from what the will stated?"

"Because he's a greedy jackass, and that's what I pretty much told him."

"I just hope he doesn't make this into some legal issue."

"That's why we have attorneys on retainer." Dallas checked his watch. "Looks like it's dinnertime, and that means your girlfriend probably isn't coming."

"No big deal."

Dallas smirked. "Yeah, right. That's why you look so damn disappointed."

He'd obviously been too transparent. "You're full of it, Dallas."

"You're foolin' yourself, baby brother."

"Am not."

"Are, too."

His frustration began to build. "I really don't care if she shows up or not."

When the bell rang, Austin shot off the chair, strode through the hallway leading to the den, then stopped short before going any farther. Truth was, he had no idea who might be at the door. Probably one of the hands. Maybe even a neighbor. Or a brother.

"Georgia, it's so good to see you!"

Okay, so Maria confirmed it was her. No need for him to rush into the room and have her thinking he was anxious to see her again. Even if he was.

On that thought, he took his time as he headed toward the front of the house to the sounds of excited voices. He stopped off in the kitchen, grabbed and uncapped a beer from the fridge, then continued on through the dining room where the food had been laid out like a banquet. He paused at the arched opening to take a drink and watch the women circling Georgie, bombarding her with compliments and questions. He wouldn't blame her if she backed out the door and left for the sake of her sanity.

Jenny glanced over her shoulder and smiled at him. "Oh, Austin, sugar, she is just precious," she said, like she'd been presented a puppy.

Then the feminine wall parted, revealing a full view of the revered guest dressed in a pale blue sweater and jeans tucked into knee-high boots. Her long, black hair, gathered up on top and secured in a clip, fell around her shoulders in soft curls.

Precious wasn't the description that came to Austin's mind. *Sexy* was much more like it. She might be small in stature, but she had an abundance of curves that would kill a lesser man. He'd had the good fortune to explore that territory on more than one occasion. He'd like to do a little exploring tonight. Slowly. With his mouth.

He felt the stirrings down south, thanks to his sinful thoughts, and realized if he didn't get a grip, he'd have to step outside.

Austin took another swig of beer and moved forward. "Glad you could come."

She sent him an overly sweet smile. "I wouldn't have missed good home cooking for the world."

Maria hooked an arm through Georgie's. "*Mija*, you are welcome anytime. Now let's go have a seat."

"Let's," Jenny said. "We don't want the food to get cold."

Austin didn't want to sit through the upcoming interrogation, but it was too late to turn back now. After all, Georgie might need a protector. Nah. She could hold her own better than most.

"I'll go get Dallas," Paris said as they wandered toward the dining room.

Austin trailed behind the threesome, all the while watching the sway of Georgie's hips. She had a butt that wouldn't quit, and he better quit thinking about that butt or he'd have to stay at the table long after dinner was done.

Jenny gestured toward the place at the head of the table. "Georgie, you sit here since you're the guest of honor."

Georgie looked a little flustered. "That's not necessary. I've sat at this table many times before."

Maria pulled out the chair. "Tonight it's necessary, *mija*. Like Jenny said, you're a special guest, even if you are practically family. We're all about hospitality around here."

"So true," Jenny said. "I came here for a weekend to let Fort meet his brothers, and I haven't gone back to Louisiana since."

"No matter how many times I've asked her to go," Maria muttered.

Jenny frowned. "Hush up, Maria. You know you like me being here to help out with the place."

"She likes your mint juleps," Austin added.

Maria hinted at a smile. "Bad as I hate to admit it, those would be hard to give up."

Following a spattering of laughter, Georgie took a seat while Maria and Jenny claimed the chairs on either side of her. Austin held back until Paris and Dallas came in and chose the two of the three remaining spots, leaving him the space at the opposite end of the table from Georgie.

He settled in, set his beer aside and eventually passed his plate to Jenny, who took great pleasure in serving the masses every night. She heaped enough food on it to feed the entire town and handed it back to him. "Do you need another beer, sugar?"

"No, thanks. I'm fine." Actually, he wouldn't be fine unless he downed a bottle of whiskey, or poured a bucket of ice down his jeans.

Georgie took a bite and just watching that ordinary gesture sparked Austin's imagination. After she dabbed at her mouth with a napkin, she asked, "I'm sorry Houston and Tyler aren't here tonight."

"They're at a rodeo in Waco," Dallas said. "Houston's determined to get one more national championship, and Tyler's there to pick up the pieces."

"Hush, *mijo*," Maria cautioned. "You'll curse your brother with such talk."

"He's already cursed," Austin added. "And if he gets one more concussion—"

"Boys," Jenny began, "you're upsetting your mothers. Now let's talk about something more pleasant." She turned her smile on Georgie. "I heard at the beauty salon that you're living at the McGregor place."

She glanced at Austin before returning her attention to Jenny. "Yes, I am. The family was nice enough to lease it to me after Liam went into the nursing home. They're not quite ready to sell the place."

Austin had a hard time believing she hadn't moved back into the Romero homestead. He figured there had to be a story behind it. "Did your mom and dad turn your room into a gym while you were gone?"

She took a drink of iced tea and set the glass down a little harder than necessary. "No. I'm an adult and I prefer to be on my own."

Jenny reached over and touched her hand. "Of course you do, but it's good to keep family close."

"As long as it's not too close," Dallas muttered, earning him a dirty look from his wife. "Speaking of family, where is Worthless?"

Jenny scowled at Dallas. "He's heading back from South Padre Island so he's running a little late. And would you please stop calling him that?" She smiled at Georgie. "You would just love Worth, sugar. How old are you?"

"Did you leave your filter in the kitchen, Jenny?" Maria asked.

"It's okay," Georgie said. "I'm thirty-four."

"Worth is twenty-nine, but five year's difference isn't bad," Jenny added. "I think it's okay for you two to date."

"It's not okay with me," Austin blurted without thought. When everyone stared at him, he had to dig himself out of the hole he'd created. "I mean, Georgie's a nice woman. Worth likes to chase nice women, but he's not the settling down kind."

Georgie lifted her chin. "Just to clarify, I'm not in the market for marriage at this point in time. Actually, I'm really too busy to date. But thanks for the offer, Jenny. I still look forward to meeting him."

"You might want to wear full-body armor," Austin muttered.

Maria stood, plate in hand. "Who wants peach cobbler?"

"I definitely do," Georgie said as she came to her feet. "I'll help you bring it in."

The pair left the kitchen and when they returned, Georgie approached Austin and set the dessert in front of him, inadvertently brushing his arm in the process. That simple touch made him shift in his seat, especially when he got a whiff of her subtle perfume. He remembered that lavender scent well. He also remembered how her hair felt brushing across his chest and lower...

Damn, damn, damn.

After everyone was served, the conversation turned casual, while Austin kept his focus on Georgie and the way her mouth caressed the fork.

Caressed the fork?

Man, he needed to get a grip. He needed some kind of distraction. Something to take his mind off Georgie.

"Hey, folks, what did I miss?"

Worth showing up was not what Austin had in mind. He glanced at Georgie, who stared at him, midbite. He could imagine what she was thinking— where did this overly buff, tanned blond guy fit into the family tree?"

"You missed dinner, Surfer Worth," Paris said. "How's the yacht?"

He walked behind Jenny's chair, leaned over and kissed her cheek. "The *Jenny Belle* is fine. How is baby Calloway?"

Paris patted her belly. "Growing like a pasture weed."

"I see that." Worth slapped Dallas on the back. "Looks like the lodge is almost finished. I'm champing at the bit to see it in its finished state."

"We still have a couple of months before that happens," Paris said.

Austin held his breath while hoping Worth made a hasty exit before he noticed Georgie.

Jenny scooted back from the table and stood.

"Sugar, we have someone we'd like you to meet," she said, shattering Austin's hopes. "This is Georgie, a longtime family friend."

Worth leveled his gaze on Georgie, grinned and eyed her like she was a prize heifer. "Where have you been hiding out?"

"College Station," Georgie answered. "Going to college."

"Veterinarian school," Dallas added. "She's going to be taking care of our livestock."

Worth moved closer to Georgie. Too close for Austin's comfort. "Then I guess I'll be seeing a lot more of you."

The veiled innuendo sent Austin from his seat. "Cut it out, Worth."

The man had the nerve to look shocked. "Cut what out?"

"Treating Georgie like she's one of your conquests."

Worth streaked a hand over his jaw. "Relax, brother. I'm just being hospitable."

Jenny patted his cheek. "Just like his mama taught him."

Maria rose and began gathering the empty plates. "Before the brawl starts, I need to clear out your Grandma Calloway's good china."

Dallas and Paris stood at the same time. "There won't be any brawl," Dallas said. "We're going to go outside and act like civil humans, not animals."

Georgie pushed back from the table and grabbed her glass. "I'll clean up."

"Or the boys could clean up," Paris began, "and we'll go out on the porch."

Maria shook her head. "We tried that one time. Their idea of a clean kitchen leaves a lot to be desired. It took me a good hour to get the grease off the stove and rewash the pots and pans. If we all help, we'll get it done faster."

"You two mothers should join the boys," Paris said. "Georgie and I will take care of this. That gives us a chance to get to know each other better."

"I don't believe the boys need a chaperone," Jenny added.

"They might need a referee." Maria rounded the table and came to Austin's side. "Come on, Jenny. We could use the break and we also need to discuss some ranch business."

Austin wasn't in the mood to discuss business with his brothers and mothers. That would mean leaving Georgie alone with his sister-in-law to most likely discuss him. But if he protested, he would wind up catching hell from everyone over his presumed *attraction* to Georgie. Okay, real attraction to Georgie. He'd go along with the plan for now, but later, he had other plans for the lady…provided she was game.

Who the hell was he trying to fool? If he laid one hand on her, she'd probably throw a right hook. Not that the prospect of getting punched would keep him from trying. First, he had to get this little family meeting over with, and then he would put the Georgie plan into action.

"Do you have plans for the upcoming weekend, Georgie?"

She took the last plate from Paris and put it in the dishwasher. "Maybe I'll unpack a box or two." Or maybe she'd just sit around with a glass of wine and mope.

Paris wiped her hands on the dish towel, hung it on the rack near the sink, then leaned back against the marble countertop. "You should come here for the festival."

"Festival?"

"I'm surprised Austin didn't mention it."

He hadn't mentioned anything other than old memories. "We haven't been together that long." And that sounded suspect. "*Together* as in the same room, not *together* together."

Paris smiled. "No need to explain. I already know you and Austin were an item in high school."

More like idiots. "Yes, we were. Now what about this festival?"

"Well, Jenny came up with the concept when she decided to leave Louisiana behind and move here. We decorate the entire place and open the ranch to the public from the second to the last week in December. It's family entertainment and it's affordable."

"How much?"

"Free."

Very surprising. The Calloways she'd always known were in the business of making money, not giving the goods away. "Seriously?"

"Seriously. Admission is the price of a toy, but that's voluntary. No one is turned away."

"That's very generous. And it includes a festival?"

"Actually, the festival is invitation-only and all the proceeds from ticket sales go to shelters in the region. We have a lot of the local ranchers attending, and several rodeo champions, along with a few San Antonio VIPs with big bucks. The food is complimentary, but we have a cash bar for safety reasons."

"Good idea. Free booze and rowdy cowboys is a surefire recipe for disaster."

"Hunky cowboys," Paris said with a smile. "I'd like to claim I haven't noticed a few in town, but I've discovered pregnancy does not render you blind. It does mess with your hormones. Just ask my husband. He told me the other night I was wearing him out."

Georgie did recall the hormone rush, and no place to go to take care of them. "I suppose you could say the D Bar C has its share of hunks."

"True, and I suspect we'll see several other sexy men this weekend from all walks of life. So if you're available, please come. And you don't have to worry about buying the ticket. It's my treat. I could use all the support I can get."

Georgie could use a night out, and since her son wouldn't be returning until three days before Christmas, she had no prior engagements. Yet she had to consider the Austin element… "I'll definitely think about attending, as long as something work-related doesn't come up."

"I'll send good thoughts that no emergencies arise." Paris laid her palm on her abdomen. "However, if I get any bigger between now and then, I'm going to need a wide-load sign to wear with my maternity cocktail dress."

Georgie smiled, remembering how she had felt that same way during her own pregnancy. "Stop it. You look great. When are you due?"

"Mid-January, as best we can tell from the ultrasound. I'm not exactly sure when I got pregnant. I found out the morning Dallas and I married the second time."

"Second time?"

Paris laughed. "It's a rather strange tale. The first time we married for all the wrong reasons. I needed a job and Dallas needed a wife before his birthday to keep control of the ranch, thanks to J.D.'s stipulation in the will. As it turned out, my ex-husband lied to me about my divorce being finalized. Dallas threatened him, I quit my position as designer for the new lodge and then he realized he couldn't live without me, so we married in earnest. End of story."

And quite a story it was. "I'm glad it worked out for you both."

"So am I." Paris flinched. "I swear, Junior here is playing soccer with my rib cage. Dallas is always asking me if the baby's kicking so he can feel it."

"Do you mind if I do?"

"Not at all, and thanks for asking. I've had complete strangers coming up to me in the store and patting my belly like a pet without my permission."

Georgie laid her palm over the place Paris had indicated, and received a tap as a reward. "Wow," she said after she moved her hand away. "Definitely a strong little guy. Or girl. Do you know the gender yet?"

Paris shook her head. "We've decided to be surprised."

"Any names picked out?"

"If it's a girl, Carlie. And if it's a boy, Luke."

"Please tell me that Luke isn't the short version of Luckenbach to carry on the tradition of naming the kids after Texas cities."

Paris grinned. "Funny you should mention that. Dallas thought it would be clever to name him Luckenbach, which I immediately nixed since it would be difficult for a child to spell it. Of course, he then came up with a whole alternate list, including Midland, Odessa, Arlington and the crowning glory, Tex-arkana."

"Glad you decided on Luke and Carlie."

They exchanged a laugh followed by Paris pressing her palms in her lower back. "These spasms are not fun."

"I remember that pain and pressure. It makes it very hard to sleep, especially when it's coupled with having to go to the bathroom five times a..." Her words trailed off when she realized she'd completely given herself away.

Paris raised a brow. "Sounds to me like you've had some experience with pregnancy."

She saw no reason to lie to Paris at this point, at least about her child's existence. "Actually, I have a five-year-old son."

Paris's eyes went wide. "I didn't know that."

"Aside from my mother and father, no one around here knows."

"Not even the Calloways?"

"Not yet." But if all went as planned, they would eventually know... As soon as she figured out how to tell the father.

"What about your son's dad?" Paris lowered her gaze. "I'm sorry. I'm being too nosy."

"It's okay. I appreciate having someone to talk to. He hasn't been in the picture."

"I'm so sorry, Georgie. I hate it when a man doesn't take responsibility for his child."

"He doesn't know."

Once more, Paris looked stunned. "Why?"

"It's complicated." More than anyone would ever know.

Paris sent her a sympathetic look. "I can do complicated, but only if you want to talk about it."

Although she'd only known Paris for an hour, Georgie sensed she could be objective, and nonjudgmental. Not to mention she'd kept the truth bottled up far too long. "When I found out I was pregnant, I tried to contact him and discovered he'd recently married. I didn't want to rock that boat."

"Is he someone you met in college?"

"No. He's from around here. That's one of the reasons I decided to return here to set up my practice. I needed to be close to my family, as well."

"Then you plan to involve him in your son's life."

She hadn't even planned how she would tell him. "Whether or not that's an option would solely be dependent on his attitude. He's not going to be thrilled that I've kept him in the dark for so long."

Paris remained silent for a few seconds, as if she needed time to digest the information. "Georgie," she began, "do the Calloways know this mystery man?"

She hesitated a moment to mull over how she would answer, and how much she would reveal. "Everyone knows everybody around here."

Paris turned and began to fold a dish towel. "Okay. It's not Dallas, is it?"

"Heavens no." Georgie realized the comment was borderline rude. "Don't get me wrong, Dallas is an attractive man, but he's always treated me like a kid sister."

Paris laid a palm on Georgie's arm. "I wasn't exactly serious. I can tell there's nothing between you two. Which leads me to another question. It's your decision whether to answer or not."

Georgie braced for the query. "Ask away."

Paris leaned back against the counter and studied her straight on. "Is it Austin?"

Georgie studied the toe of her boot. "Well…uh… I…"

"I know you two have been involved before," Paris continued. "And I can tell you still care about him by the way you look at him."

If Paris had noticed, what about the rest of the Calloways? What about Austin? Had she really been that obvious? "Yes, I cared about him a lot a long time ago, and in some ways I still do. Unfortunately I made the fatal mistake of letting those feelings get in the way of logic six years ago."

"Then if you do still care about him, Georgie, you should tell him you have a child together."

"I never actually said he's the father."

"You haven't denied it, either."

Georgie resigned herself to the fact that she

couldn't get out of this predicament without digging a deeper deception hole. "All right. Austin is Chance's father. We got together the night after the reading of his father's will. He was upset when he learned about J.D.'s double life, and I wanted so badly to comfort him. That's how we conceived our son."

Paris sent her a sympathetic look. "Austin is a good man. He'll understand why you felt you couldn't tell him at that point in time."

If only she could believe that theory. "I had every intention of telling him, but when I found out he was married, I didn't have the heart to mess up his life. At the time it seemed like the right thing to do. But when I learned he was divorced right before I finished vet school, I realized maybe I'd been wrong. Now he's going to hate me for not telling him sooner."

"He's going to be angry, but I doubt he'll hate you. And I know he won't hate having a son. That's why I believe you should let him know, unless you plan to keep your son hidden until he's an adult."

She needed more time to think. She needed to get home before her mom called.

With that in mind, Georgie turned to Paris and attempted a small smile. "I'm going to take everything you've said into serious consideration. In the meantime, if you don't mind—"

"Not saying anything to anyone?" Paris returned her smile. "I promise I won't mention it, and after you've told Austin, I'll pretend to be as surprised as everyone else."

"After you've told me what, Georgie?"

Three

Georgie startled at the sound of Austin's voice, so much so she physically jumped. "We were talking about…uh… We were playing a game."

He tossed the beer can in the recycle bin and frowned. "What kind of game?"

"A guessing game," Paris said. "Georgie tells me a story from your childhood, and I have to guess which brother did what."

Georgie thanked her lucky stars Paris had such a sharp mind. "That's right. I just mentioned the time someone was doing donuts in the Parkers' pasture. I told her everyone thought it was Dallas, when it was really you, and she thought I should tell you to confess to Dallas to clear the air." And that had to be the lamest fabrication ever to leave her mouth.

He strolled farther into the kitchen and frowned. "Yep, that was me doing the donuts on the night after I found out I got accepted into college. And FYI, Dallas already knows. He took the blame because he knew Dad would come down harder on me."

Georgie recalled that fateful day when Austin had informed her about his college acceptance, and she had assumed he would be out of her life forever. Now just the opposite would be true, if she told him about Chance.

She did a quick check of her watch and saw an excuse to escape both Austin's and Paris's questions. "It's time for me to go. I have to be up very early in the morning to make my rounds."

"I'll walk you out," Austin said.

"Thanks, but I can make it to the truck on my own. Finish your visit with the family."

"I see the family almost every day and Mom would skin me alive if I wasn't gentlemanly." Austin turned around and headed away. "I'll wait for you on the porch."

Great. Just great. The man was as persistent as a gnat on a banana.

Paris drew Georgie into a brief hug. "I've enjoyed our talk. Let's do it again very soon."

Georgie didn't have to ask what they would be

discussing. "That sounds like a plan. Maybe we can have lunch."

"Lunch would be great. And I know you're going to do the right thing and eventually clear the air, once and for all."

That's exactly what Georgie intended to do. She simply wasn't sure when, where or, most important, how.

Now was not the time. Georgie recognized that reality the moment she stepped onto the porch and met a swarm of Calloways bombarding her with goodbyes.

Jenny gave her the first hug. "Please come again soon, sugar. I'll make my juleps."

"You'll make her drunk," Maria said as she gave Georgie a quick embrace, as well. "It's been good to see you, *mija*."

"Don't be a stranger," Dallas added as he patted her back like the brother he'd always been to her.

Worth stepped forward, kissed her hand and grinned. "Call me sometime and we'll hang out."

"When he's not hanging ten on a surfboard," Jenny said.

"Or hanging out in town, trying to pick up women," Dallas remarked.

"Yeah, all three of them," Worth said.

The comment earned some laughter from everyone but the man leaning back against the railing, arms folded across his chest, his blue eyes boring into Georgie. She waited until the crowd reentered the house before she moved forward, seeking a quick getaway.

Unfortunately Austin had other ideas, she realized when he clasped her arm before she made it down the first step. "Where are you going so fast?"

She turned a serious gaze on him and he relinquished his grasp on her. "I'm heading home. It's getting late."

"Are you sure you don't want to hang around a little longer and tell me what's going on with you?"

Hey, I had a baby over five years ago and he happens to be yours. Just thought you might like to know. "Nothing's going on, Austin, other than I'm tired. As I said earlier, I have to be up at dawn."

He pushed off the rail and moved close enough to almost shatter her composure. "You're as nervous as a colt in a corral full of cows. I can't help but think it has something to do with me."

He would be right. "Check your ego at the door, Austin. Not everything has to do with you. Now if you don't mind, I'm leaving."

She sprinted down the remaining steps and quickened her pace as she headed down the walkway without looking back. When she reached her silver truck, she grasped the handle only to have a large hand prevent her from opening the door.

Frustrated, she turned around and practically bumped into Austin's chest. "What is it now?"

"Before you run off, I wanted to ask you something."

"Okay, but make it quick."

"We're having a party here this weekend and—"

"Paris invited me."

"Are you going to come?"

With the cowboy in such close proximity, his palm planted above her head on the door, she could barely think, much less make a decision. "I'm not sure. It depends on my schedule."

His grin arrived as slow as honey and just as sweet, with a hint of deviousness. "It's been a long time since we've danced together."

"True, and I've probably forgotten how."

He took a lock of her hair and began to slowly twist it around his finger, as he had done so many times before. "Do you remember that barn dance back when we were in high school? Specifically, what happened afterward?"

Here we go again… "I recall several dances back in the day."

"The one right before my graduation, when we fogged up all the windows in my truck while we were parked down by the creek."

He seemed determined to yank her back down memory mile. "It wasn't all that monumental, Austin. Only some minor teenage petting."

"Minor? You were so hot you took my hand and put it right between your legs."

"I don't exactly remember it that way." One whopper of a lie.

"Do you remember that you didn't stop me from undoing your pants and slipping my hand inside? I sure as hell haven't forgotten, even if you have."

A woman never forgot her first climax. "Your point?"

"I definitely had a *point* below my belt buckle," he said, his voice low and grainy. "I went home with it that night, and several times after that until the night before I left for college."

Ah, yes, another enchanted evening…and one colossal mistake. "That should never have happened, Austin. I didn't plan to give you my virginity as a high school graduation gift."

"But what a gift it was." He leaned over and brushed a kiss across her cheek. "I liked the sports socks, but not as much."

"Not funny," she said as she unsuccessfully tried to repress a smile.

"Seriously, Georgie girl, don't you ever believe I didn't appreciate what that night meant to you, and me. I've never wanted you to think I took it for granted."

Over the past few years, she'd managed to suppress those particular recollections. But now, they came rushing back on a tide of unforgettable moments. "I know you didn't, Austin. You apologized to me a million times, not to mention you were so gentle. When it comes right down to it, I'm glad it was you, and not some jerk bent on bragging to all his friends that he nailed the school wallflower."

"Wallflower?" He released a low, rough laugh. "Georgie, you were anything but a wallflower. Every girl wanted to be just like you, every guy in high school lusted after you and because you wouldn't give those guys the time of day, that made you all the more attractive."

Like she really believed that. "I highly doubt anyone was lusting after me, and even if they did, I was too busy maintaining a secret relationship with you."

"We still had some good times, didn't we?"

"Yes, we did." Something suddenly occurred to her. "Did you ever tell anyone about us?"

He glanced away before returning his gaze to her. "Dallas knew. He told me several times we were playing with fire and we were going to get burned if either of our dads found out. Did you tell anyone?"

She shook her head. "No." Not until she'd found out she was pregnant, and then she'd only revealed the secret to her mother. "I didn't dare."

Georgie's cell phone began to vibrate and after she fished it from her pocket, she discovered Lila on the line, as if she'd channeled her mom. "I need to take this, so I better go."

Austin pushed away from the truck but didn't budge. "I'll wait."

She couldn't have a conversation with her son

while Austin stood by, staring at her. That became a moot point when she noticed the call had already ended. "It's just my mom checking in from Florida. I'll get back to her when I'm home."

"Good. I've enjoyed talking to you again, just like old times."

Fortunately talking hadn't turned into something more, just like old times. "I've enjoyed it, too, but I really do need to go."

"Before you go, there's something I just have to do."

She pointed at him. "Don't even think about it."

He had the nerve to look innocent. "Think about what?"

"You know what."

"No, I don't. I was going to give you my cell number, in case you need anything."

Feeling a little foolish, she opened the contacts list and handed him her phone. "Fine. Plug it in there. But hurry."

He typed in his number, then handed the cell back. She laughed when she noticed he'd labeled himself "Studly," the name she jokingly used to call him. "Very clever."

"Can I have your number?"

"I'll text it to you."

"Can I have one more thing?"

She released a weary sigh. "What now?"

"This."

He framed her face in his palms and covered her mouth with his before she had time to issue a protest. She knew she should pull away, but as it had always been, she was completely captive to the softness of his lips, the gentle stroke of his tongue, his absolute skill. No one had ever measured up to him when it came to kissing. She suspected no one ever would.

Once they parted, Austin tipped his forehead against hers. "Man, I've missed this."

Sadly so had she. "We're not children anymore, Austin. We can't go back to the way it was."

He took an abrupt step back. "I'm not suggesting we do that. But we can go forward, see where it goes."

"It won't go anywhere because you'll never be able to give me what I want."

"What do you want, Georgie?"

"More."

"How much more?"

"I want it all. Marriage, a home and family."

"I've gone the marriage route, and I blew it. I don't want to travel that path again."

She turned and opened her truck door. "Then it's probably best that we stay away from each other."

"Is that what you really want?"

Her head said yes, while her heart said no. "Right now I want to go to bed."

He grinned like the cad he could be. "Mine's just down the road a bit. A big king-size bed with a top-grade mattress made of memory foam. A good place to make a few more memories."

She tossed her phone on the passenger seat, withdrew the key from her pocket and started the truck. "Good night, Austin."

"Night, Georgie. And if you change your mind about us exploring our options, just let me know."

"Don't count on it."

When she tried to close the door, he stopped her again. "Just one more question. Are you still worried about what your folks would think if they knew we were together?"

In many ways, she was. "If we started seeing each other again, and I'm not saying that will happen, I'm sure my father would go ballistic. I'm fairly certain my mother wouldn't care what we do together."

"Georgia May, have you taken leave of your senses?"

Georgie collapsed onto the bed and sighed. "I went there to see the family, Mom. Just because you've never cared for the Calloways because of that stupid dispute between J.D. and Dad, doesn't mean I don't like them. They've always been nice to me."

"I assume Austin was there."

"Yes, he was."

"You didn't tell him about Chance, did you?"

The panic in her mother's voice wasn't lost on Georgie. "No, not yet."

"I don't think you should tell him."

Georgie couldn't be more confused. "But you told me right before the trip that you thought I should tell him."

"I've changed my mind. Your father agrees with me."

A strong sense of trepidation passed through her. "Dad knows Austin is Chance's father?"

"Not exactly, but he has his suspicions. Regardless, we think it's better if you remain silent to avoid any disappointment for both you and Chance."

They'd been having this back-and-forth conversation since she'd told her mother about the baby. "Mom, we've been through this a thousand times. I'm going to do what's best for my child, not to mention Dad has no say-so in the decision. He refuses to even acknowledge he has a grandson. He's barely spoken to me for the past six years."

"I know, sweetie, but—"

"Where are you now?" she said in an effort to move off the subject.

"Alabama for the night. We'll be in Florida tomorrow afternoon."

"Is Chance doing okay?"

"He's been an angel. Right now he's outside with Ben and Deb hooking up the RV. He's so inquisitive."

Georgie wouldn't debate that, and her son's curiosity about his father had begun to increase by leaps and bounds with every passing year. "Do you mind putting him on the phone? It's getting late."

"All right. Hold on a minute."

"Mom, before you go, I just wanted to say how much I've appreciated your support. I couldn't have raised my baby boy without your guidance. I love you for it."

"I love you, too, dear, and I only want what's best for you and Chance. If that means you decide that telling Austin he's a father is best, then so be it."

She was simply too befuddled to make any serious decisions right now.

A few moments later, she heard the muffled patter of footsteps, followed by, "Hi, Mom. I have my own bed and we have a kitchen. Uncle Ben showed me how to plug in the 'lectricity and roll down that big thing over the door so we don't get sunburned. It's so cool."

She could imagine her son rocking back and forth on his heels, his hazel eyes wide with wonderment. "It sounds great, baby. It's way past your bedtime. You must be tired."

"Nope. We're gonna roast marshmallows."

Lovely. Her child was being exposed to electricity and fire. "Be very careful, Chance. I don't want you to hurt yourself."

"Aw, Mom, I'm not a baby."

No, he wasn't. "You're still my baby. I love you, ya know."

"Love ya, too, you know. Gotta go now."

"Don't stay up too late and—"

When the call cut off, Georgie's heart sank. How would she survive the next two weeks without him? By keeping herself occupied with work. By having lunch with Paris. Maybe she would even attend the Calloways' party.

And perhaps she would finally get off the fence and tell Austin he had a son. She worried he already suspected something was up.

As sure as the sun would rise in the east, Austin sensed Georgie was hiding something. Then again, she'd always been one to hold back.

He strode into the den, grabbed the remote and started to watch a replay of his last national championship roping. But the thought of revisiting that part of his past didn't seem all that appealing. He'd rather relive another part.

On that thought, he pulled down the yearbook, dropped into the brown leather chair by the fireplace and flipped through the pages until he reached the class photo of Georgie. She'd been a junior, he'd been a senior, and they'd been secretly hot and heavy that whole year.

Funny, she hadn't changed all that much. Her hair was still as long, her face still as beautiful, her brown eyes still as enticing. She could never see what everyone had seen in her—a perfect blend of her Spanish/Scottish heritage.

She hadn't been a cheerleader or a drill team member. She'd been a rodeo girl through and through, friends with many, and more popular than she'd realized until she'd been elected homecoming queen her senior year. And class president. And eventually, prom queen. During all those milestone moments, he'd been away at college, never serving as her escort, never revealing they had been an item in high school. He should've been horsewhipped for not standing and shouting it from the rooftop when he'd had the chance, their fathers and distance be damned. He should have been there for her.

Too late now, he thought as he closed the book and set it aside on the mahogany end table. He couldn't help but think his life might have been different if he'd stayed home six years ago instead of moving back to Vegas.

He recalled that last night with Georgie, when her touch had temporarily eased his anger over learning about his father's deceit. They'd made love until dawn, then parted ways. And then he'd met Abby, married in a matter of months and ended it without much thought. Not that it could have been any other way. Not when Georgia May Romero still weighed on his mind on a regular basis. Abby hadn't known about her, but she'd always claimed she'd never had all of his heart. She would have been right.

Now he found himself reunited with Georgie. Together again, to quote an old country song. Nope, not exactly together. If Georgie had her way, he'd fall off the face of the earth, or go back to Nevada. But damn, she had kissed him back. And damn, he wanted to kiss her again. Maybe that wouldn't be fair in light of their opposing goals—he wanted to stay single, she wanted to be a wife.

If he had any sense, he'd grow up, get with the program and open himself to all the possibilities. But the thought of failing Georgie, not being the man she needed, battered him with doubts.

But the thought of having her so close, and not being with her again, didn't sit well with him. He would just keep his options open whenever he saw her again. And he damn sure planned to see her again.

Four

When she maneuvered through the D Bar C's iron gate, Georgie pulled behind several slow-moving, white limos as they traveled down the lane leading to the party site. She marveled at the complete transformation of the Calloway ranch.

The lawn of the main house to her left had been laden with various decorations depicting holidays from around the world. Every tree and hedgerow had been draped with twinkling lights, and laser beams in rotating colors sparkled across its facade. Several cartoon characters and giant candy canes lined the curbs on either side of the street, enhancing the fairy-tale quality.

Georgie passed by three more massive houses set back from the road, all adorned like the first, and she wondered if one of the cedar-and-rock houses belonged to Austin. She hadn't bothered to ask him the other night for fear he might get the wrong idea, but she couldn't deny her curiosity.

She also couldn't deny her building excitement as the caravan turned to the right to reveal a large silvery tent set out at the end of the road, a two-story residence, bigger than any she'd seen to this point, serving as its backdrop.

Georgie came to a complete stop when a parking attendant, dressed in a tuxedo and cowboy hat, approached her. She shut off the ignition, grabbed her silver clutch that complemented her sleeveless black dress, draped her silk wrap around her shoulders and slid out of the cab.

The valet offered her a long once-over and a somewhat lecherous grin. "What's a beautiful little thing like you driving a big ol' truck like this? You belong in a limo."

You belong back at college, frat boy. "My big ol' boyfriend owns this big ol' truck."

He looked unfazed by the threatening lie. "He's an idiot for letting you attend this little get-together all by your lonesome."

"He had to work."

"Oh, yeah? What does he do?"

She handed him her keys, a ten-dollar tip and

another tall tale. "He's a professional wrestler. Take good care of his truck."

With that, she turned on her spiky black heels and carefully made her way to the party. Once inside the tent, she navigated the milling crowd, past tables filled with sophisticated finger foods and prissy desserts, searching for a familiar face among the strangers. Luckily she spotted two familiar faces positioned near the makeshift dance floor. With Paris wearing a flowing green empire-waist dress barely showing her belly, her blond hair cascading in soft curls around her bare shoulders, and Dallas decked out in a black suit, complete with red tie and dark cowboy hat, they looked as if they belonged on the cover of a trendy fashion magazine...or a bridal cake. A fortysomething man with a hint of gray at his temples stood across from the couple. Most women would label him debonair. From the looks of the expensive suit and high-dollar watch, Georgie would label him wealthy.

After Paris waved her over, Georgie wandered toward them, hoping she hadn't inadvertently interrupted some sort of business deal.

Paris immediately left her husband's side and greeted Georgie with a hug. "You look beautiful, Georgie."

She nervously tugged at the dress's crisscross halter neck that felt a bit like a noose. "Thanks. I

haven't worn anything like this since my college senior spring formal a dozen years ago."

Paris looked surprised. "You're thirty-three?"

"Actually, thirty-four."

"I swear you could go to a high school dance right
now and blend right in. And that is not a bad thing."

*Unless I tried to purchase a glass of wine with-
out being asked for my ID.* "That's nice of you to
say, but the only thing that might help me pass for
a student happens to be my height. My dad used to
call me 'Peanut.'" And now he wouldn't even acknowledge her as his daughter. The thought damp-
ened her mood.

"Don't discount your beauty," Paris said. "Every
man in the room, from twenty-one to eighty-one,
would like to take you home."

Yeah, sure. "I'm flattered, but I don't believe it."

"Hello. I'm Rich Adler. Who are you?"

Georgie turned her attention to the man behind
the introduction. The same man who'd been convers-
ing with Dallas. She found his name both ironic and
appropriate. "Georgia Romero," she said as she took
his offered hand for a brief shake.

Dallas moved forward as if running interference.
"Rich is an attorney. He also owns a quarter horse
operation outside San Antonio."

The lawyer sent her a somewhat seedy smile. "I'm
into breeding."

She resisted rolling her eyes. "I'm sure that keeps you busy."

"Not as busy as I'd like," he said. "Dallas tells me you're a veterinarian."

"Yes, I am."

He winked. "I could use a good vet."

She could use a quick exit. "I'm sure you have several options in the city."

"Not any who look as good as you. Have you ever been to Italy?"

She sent him an overly sweet and somewhat sarcastic smile. "Oh, yes. That nice little town right outside Hillsboro. I passed by it once on the interstate on my way to Oklahoma."

Now he looked perplexed. "I'm referring to the country, not the town in Texas."

She started to mention she was kidding, but she suspected his arrogance trumped any true sense of humor. "'Fraid not."

He had the gall to move closer. "You would enjoy it there. Extraordinary cuisine and superior wine. The Amalfi coast is a great place to don your bikini and sunbathe. Do you have a passport?"

She had a strong urge to back up and run. "Passport, yes. Bikini, no. I do have a very busy practice to run. No time for vacations." Even if she did, she had no desire to travel with him.

Dallas cleared his throat and slapped randy Rich

on the back. "Let me buy you a drink, Adler, and we'll leave the ladies to talk about us."

Georgie planned to do just that, and she would have nothing flattering to say about the lecherous lawyer. "Nice to meet you, Mr. Adler." Not.

"It's Rich." He pulled a card and pen from his inside pocket, jotted something down, then handed it to her. "If you need a job, here's my info."

She wouldn't work for him if he happened to be the last employer on earth. "Have a good night."

He leaned over and murmured, "Call me. For business or pleasure."

Oh, she'd like to call him…several names that wouldn't be fit to utter in this atmosphere.

As soon as the men left the area, Paris turned to Georgie. "I'm so, so sorry. That guy is a first-class jerk."

As far as Georgie was concerned, that was a colossal understatement. "A jerk and a creep."

"A married, creepy jerk."

Georgie wadded up the card and tossed it into a nearby waste bin. "Figures."

"He's on his fourth wife."

"What a shocker. I could have gone all night without meeting the likes of him."

When a roving waiter passed by, Paris snatched a crystal tumbler from his tray and offered it to Georgie. "Drink this. It might help erase the memory."

Georgie took the glass and held it up. "What is this?"

"It's Jenny's infamous mint julep. She made several gallons' worth to go with the champagne."

She eyed the dark gold liquid for a moment. "Does she use a lot of bourbon?"

"Yes, and a splash of rum and she adds tequila for a little extra kick."

"Interesting." Georgie took a sip and found it to be surprisingly palatable, albeit extremely strong. "Wow. This will wake you up today and give you a headache tomorrow."

Paris leaned over, lowered her voice and said, "Take some advice. Sip it slowly, and don't have more than one, unless you have a designated driver."

"Believe me, I won't."

For the first time since her arrival, Georgie scanned the room to study the attendees…and spotted Austin standing nearby, dressed in a navy jacket, white shirt and dark jeans with a dark cowboy hat to complete the look. He had a bevy of woman hanging on his every word and wore a grin that could melt the icing off the red velvet cupcakes lined up on the stand behind him.

As bad luck would have it, he caught her looking, and when he winked, Georgie downed a little more of the julep than she should. "Still the cowboy cad," she muttered, the taste of tequila and jealousy on her tongue.

Paris frowned. "Who are you referring to?"

"Your brother-in-law. The one who's named after the capital of Texas." She nodded to her left. "He's over there, draped in women."

She followed Georgie's gaze to where Austin was surrounded by several young females who were probably quite willing to be at his beck and call. "He came here alone," Paris said. "In fact, I haven't known him to date anyone since we met."

Georgie took another ill-advised gulp. "Austin doesn't date. He passes through a girl's life, shows her a good time, then blows away like a tumbleweed."

"He dated you, didn't he?"

"Using today's teenage vernacular, we basically hooked up."

Paris remained silent for a moment before she spoke again. "Have you talked to him yet about… the issue?"

Issue as in their child. "I've been busy, and I'm waiting for the right time."

"Maybe you'll have the opportunity to speak to him tonight."

She glanced Austin's way to find his admirers had disappeared and he was now leaning back against the bar, his gaze trained on her. "Maybe I will." Maybe not.

Paris hooked her arm through Georgie's. "You'll know when the time is right. And by the way, I have a doctor's appointment Tuesday morning. After that,

I'm free for the day. Why don't you and I have lunch in San Antonio?"

Georgie could use the break and the camaraderie. "Most of my appointments are in the morning. I can probably rearrange my schedule and clear the afternoon."

"Good." Paris looked a bit distracted before she returned her attention to Georgie. "I need to go rescue my husband from the creepy jerk. I'd invite you over but—"

"No offense, but no thanks. I've had enough exposure to Rich. I'll just mingle a bit and we can catch up later."

"Sounds like a plan." Paris started away then turned around again. "Be careful with that drink."

What was left of the drink. "I will."

After her friend departed, Georgie milled around the tent, greeting a few people she'd known a while back and nodding at several strangers. She could see Austin from the corner of her eye, basically tracking her path like a cougar stalking his prey, yet keeping his distance. She felt like a walking bundle of nervous energy, and that led her to finish the drink and take another from the waiter as he walked by. She planned to only hold this one, not drink it. But when the cat-and-mouse game with Austin continued and he smiled at her, she took another sip. And then another, even with Paris's warning going off in her head like a fire alarm.

After she noticed Austin approaching her, she began to survey the silent auction offerings laid out on a lengthy table. If she ignored him, maybe he'd just go away—and that was like believing the temperature wouldn't reach one hundred degrees in South Texas next summer.

"Georgie girl, I'm going to bid on that six-horse trailer with the sleeping quarters."

The feel of his warm breath playing over her neck and the sultry sound of his voice caused her to tighten the wrap around her arms against the pleasant chills. If she turned around, she would be much too close to him, so she continued to peruse the items until she regained some composure. "The spa day looks intriguing."

"I've never had a massage for two. I'm game if you are."

She disregarded the comment and sidestepped to the next offering displayed beneath a small glass case—an exquisite oval diamond ring encircled by a multitude of sparkling rubies. "Now this is quite nice." She then noted the shocking top bid on the sheet. "Surely I'm not reading this right."

Austin leaned over her shoulder, causing her to shiver slightly and take another sip of the drink. "Yep, you are. It's twenty-thousand dollars' worth of nice. You should go for it."

She regarded him over one shoulder. "I don't believe wearing this while inoculating cattle would be practical."

"All work and no play makes for a boring life."

"As beautiful as it is, it's not me." She noticed another, less gaudy ring to her left. A simple silver setting with a round sapphire surrounded by petite diamonds. "Now that's more me, but ten thousand dollars still isn't in my budget."

"Maybe Santa will bring it to you."

Against better judgment, she pivoted around and confronted Austin head-on. "If Santa Claus, Mrs. Claus, the elves and the tooth fairy pooled their funds, I still doubt they can afford this ring."

"Then let me bid on it for you."

He'd clearly lost his mind. "Don't you dare."

He sent her a sexy, sultry grin. "I have something better to give you."

She could only guess what that entailed. "We're not going there, either, Austin."

He frowned. "Get your mind out of the gutter, Georgie. I want to give you a dance."

That took her aback. "What?"

"The band's playing a slow song. Dance with me."

"As I told you recently, I highly doubt I remember how."

"I highly doubt you could ever forget. Now put down that drink and that bag you've been hanging on to like a lifeline, and follow me onto the floor."

She scraped her mind for some excuse to prevent

her from falling into his sensual trap. "I can't just leave my purse unattended."

"What's in it?"

"My phone, driver's license, a five-dollar bill and lipstick."

"Credit cards?"

"No, but—"

"I guarantee no one in this crowd is going to steal that dinky bag, and if someone does, I'll replace your phone and the cash. You're on your own when it comes to the lipstick and driver's license."

Against better judgment, she finished off the last of the julep. "I'm holding you responsible if my *dinky* bag turns up missing."

Austin took the purse from her grasp and handed the glass off to a waiter. He then set the clutch on a table and used her wrap to cover it. "No one will even know it's there."

No one would know how needy she felt at the moment when Austin clasped her hand, either.

Unable to fight his persistence, Georgie allowed Austin to lead her onto the floor and, once there, he took her right hand into his left, wrapped his arm around her waist and pulled her close.

The slow country song spoke of lost love and long-ago memories, a fitting tribute to their past. Georgie felt a bit light-headed, and she wasn't sure if it was because of the booze, or her partner. She pressed her cheek against his chest, closed her eyes and relaxed against him. She relished the feel of his palm roving over her back, his quiet strength, his skill. The first song gave way to another, then another, and still they continued to move to the music, as if they didn't have a care in the world.

When Austin tipped her chin up, forcing her to look into those magnetic cobalt eyes, she sensed he wanted to say something. Instead, he kissed her softly, deeply, taking her breath and composure. After they parted, Georgie could only imagine what the attendees were thinking, particularly Paris and Dallas, who were standing not far away, staring at them. She also noticed the couple had been joined by a crowd of Calloways. Mothers Jenny and Maria seemed pleased, the two dark-haired brothers, Houston and Tyler, looked annoyed, and the only blond sibling, Worth, evidently found the whole scene amusing, considering his grin.

Georgie tipped her forehead against his chest. "We're going to be the talk of the town."

"So?"

She looked up at him. "So if my father finds out I was canoodling with a man in public, and that man happens to be a Calloway, it won't be good for either of us."

Austin stopped and escorted her into a secluded corner. "Georgie, it's high time you stop caring what your dad thinks. And when it comes down to it, we weren't making out on the dance floor. I just gave you a simple kiss."

A kiss that curled her toes in her stilettos. "Some would deem it inappropriate."

"*Some* can kiss my ass."

Georgie suddenly felt very warm and a tad bit dizzy. "I need some air."

Taking her by the arm, Austin guided Georgie outside the tent and set her on a wooden bench. "Better?" he asked.

She pinched the bridge of her nose and closed her eyes. "It's the drinks."

"Drinks? You had more than one of those mint juleps?"

"I know. Paris warned me, but I was…thirsty."

"You could've gotten water or a soda at the bar."

She frowned up at him. "I don't need a lecture. I need to go home."

"You're not fit to drive, Georgie."

She wouldn't debate that. "I know. Do you mind driving me home?"

"You can stay at my house."

She wasn't *that* tipsy. "Not a good idea."

"I have four bedrooms and four bathrooms. You can take your pick."

She found that odd. "Why so many?"

He shrugged. "The builder told me it was better for resale, not that anyone would buy a house in the Cowboy Commune."

Georgie giggled like a schoolgirl. "Is that what you're calling it these days?"

"That's what people around these parts have labeled it."

"I suppose it does fit."

He took both her hands and pulled her up. "Let's get your things and get you to bed."

She gave him a quelling look. "Austin Calloway—"

"A bed in a guestroom." He wrapped his arm around her waist and traveled toward the tent. "Of course, my bed is probably the best."

"Hush."

He favored her with a grin. "Okay. I'll be good."

Georgie knew how good he could be when he was being bad. For that reason, she should demand he drive her home. But all her wisdom went the way of the cool wind when he paused and gave her another kiss, and this one wasn't simple at all.

She wasn't too mentally fuzzy to know that if she didn't keep her wits about her, she would end up in Austin Calloway's bed.

"Here's the bedroom." Austin opened the door and stepped aside to allow Georgie some space to move past him. When she brushed against his belly, he realized he should've stood at the end of the hall. Or outside on the front porch.

He could hear his stepmom telling him to be a

man about it and leave her be. Unfortunately, that seemed to be his problem. What man wouldn't want to sweep this woman up and make love to her until dawn?

Don't even think about it, Calloway.

But that was all he could think about when Georgie wandered into the room, perched on the edge of the bed and ran her palm over the teal-colored comforter like she was stroking a pet. "This is a really nice room. Has anyone stayed in here before me?"

He moved into the doorway but didn't dare go farther. "Nope. You're the first. Jenny's the one who decorated the place. That's why it's so frilly."

"It's pretty. I like peacock colors." She hid a yawn behind her hand. "I want to apologize for my behavior. I didn't plan to get drunk."

"I wouldn't qualify you as drunk. In fact, in all the time I've known you, I've never even seen you have a beer."

She crossed her legs, causing the dress to shift higher, revealing some mighty nice thighs. "I've only done it once. On my twenty-first birthday, a group of my college girlfriends and I hired a limo and went bar hopping. I had several cosmopolitans and a hangover to beat all hangovers the next day. It was awful."

"We've all been there before."

She leaned back and braced herself on her elbows. "I prefer not to go there again. Do you have a spare toothbrush?"

"Yep." He pointed at the sliding door across the room. "In the bathroom. That's Jenny's doing, too. She stocked the place with everything any guest would need, male or female."

"She didn't happen to put a gown in there, did she?"

"I don't think so."

"Then can I borrow one of your T-shirts? Otherwise I won't have a thing to wear."

Damn. Just when he'd gotten his mind off seeing her naked. "Sure. I'll be right back."

He took off down the hall at a fast clip and, when he reached his bedroom closet, tugged a faded blue rodeo T-shirt off the hanger. On the way back, he gave himself a mental pep talk on the virtues of keeping his hands to himself and his mind on honor.

Georgie sent him a sleepy smile when he reentered the guestroom. "That was fast. Hand it here."

Austin almost froze in his tracks when Georgie began to fiddle with the collar at the back of her neck. Honor and virtue went down the drain when he imagined the front of the dress dropping to her waist. Maria's cautions went unheeded when he fantasized about putting his hands on her. And to make matters worse, she came to her feet and turned around, giving him a bird's-eye view of her butt. "Can you help me with this?"

Man, he'd love to, but probably not in the way she'd meant. "Help you with what?"

She held her hair up with one hand. "This bow thingie. It's in a knot."

His *gut* was in a knot, and that would be the least of his problems if he came anywhere near her.

He could do this. He could help her with the kink in her collar and ignore the one building below his belt buckle. Good thing she didn't have eyes in the back of her head.

After tossing the T-shirt on the bed, he studied the twisted bow and worried over what would happen if he managed to get it untied. "Just hang on to the dress."

"Of course I will," she said, her tone hinting at irritation.

He'd been known for his steady hands, but he actually fumbled with the tie for a time before he had it undone. "There you go. All set."

Without warning, Georgie spun around and somehow managed to whack him in the jaw with her elbow. He hadn't been at all prepared for the accidental blow, nor had he expected his inadvertent attacker to frame his face in her palms. "I'm so sorry, Austin. Did I hurt you?"

Oh, yeah, he was hurting, but it wasn't from getting smacked. Right there, in his field of vision, a man's biggest fantasy, and in his case, worst nightmare—a pair of bare breasts. Tempting, round breasts close enough to touch. He'd seen breasts before. He'd seen hers before, several times, although they looked a bit fuller than he recalled. He'd touched them before, with his hands and his mouth. Damn if he didn't want to do that now.

"Austin?"

He forced his gaze back to her face. "You forgot something."

She glanced down, then back up and her eyes went wide. "Oops."

The next oops came when he noticed *that* look, the one she'd always given him when she'd wanted a kiss. But maybe that's only what he wanted to see. Regardless, he had to maintain some control. Be a true gentleman. Hang tight to his honor.

And that plan went right out the window when she pulled him down to her lips. That's when caution gave way to chemistry. She started walking backward, taking him with her. and before he knew it, they were on the bed, facing each other with their legs twined together. He managed to remove his jacket while they continued to kiss like there was no tomorrow. She worked the buttons on his shirt and slipped her hand inside. He slid his palm slowly up the back of her thigh and continued on until he contacted a skimpy pair of silk panties.

Completely caught up in his need, Austin planted kisses down Georgie's neck and traveled to her breasts. He circled his tongue around one nipple before taking it into his mouth, using the pull of his lips to tempt her. She answered by running her hands though his hair and moving restlessly against him.

He wanted more from her. He wanted it all. But he couldn't have it unless he knew she wanted the same. On that thought, he raised his head and sought her eyes. "Before this goes any further, convince me you know what you're doing."

Unfortunately the interlude ended as quickly as it started when Georgie broke away, scrambled to her feet and pulled the top of her dress back into place. "Apparently I don't know what I'm doing since I swore this wouldn't happen again," she said, clear frustration in her voice.

Austin rolled to his back, draped an arm over his closed eyes and tried to catch his breath. "You started it."

"You didn't seem to be complaining."

"I couldn't complain with our tongues in each other's mouths."

When he heard the sound of a slamming door, Austin opened his eyes, expecting to discover Georgie had left the premises, if not the house. Instead, he noticed the bedroom door was still open, but the one leading into the bathroom had been closed.

Austin sat up and rubbed both hands over his face in a futile effort to erase the memories of their encounter. He figured he might as well leave now since he doubted she'd come out unless he made a quick exit. Obviously he'd been wrong, he realized when she walked back into the room wearing only his T-shirt and no smile.

She folded her arms around her middle and leaned back against the wall next to the door. "I'm sorry. You're not to blame for my behavior."

Regardless of blame, the damage to his libido had already been done. "I need to apologize to you. After two of Jenny's drinks, I should've realized you're not in charge of your faculties."

She crossed her arms around her middle and raised her chin. "I wasn't drunk."

"Okay. Tipsy."

"Maybe, but I'm quite sober now."

And he was still so jacked up he could pull that too-big shirt up over her ruffled hair and take her up against the wall. "And I'm betting you're tired. Have a good night. See you in the morning."

He turned on his heels and almost made it to the door before she asked, "Where are you going?"

Straight to hell if he faced her again. "To bed."

"I thought we could talk awhile."

He didn't want to talk. He wanted to get back down to business. "I'm pretty worn out," he said without moving.

"Come on, Austin. You're a night owl just like me."

He'd be hooting up a storm—or howling like a coyote—if he got anywhere near her again. "Georgie,

I'm fairly sure if I stay, I wouldn't want to use my mouth to talk, especially since you're half-dressed."

She laughed. "You've seen me in a bikini. Actually, you've seen me wearing nothing."

If she kept talking that way, she'd see the evidence of what those memories did to him. What she'd done to him a few minutes ago. He had one hell of an erection and no place to go. "I think it might be better if I go to my own room."

"Man up, Calloway. You're not a teenager anymore. You can have an adult conversation with a woman without any other expectations."

Under normal circumstance, that was a given. But with her...

Dammit, he was up for the challenge, *up* being the operative word. Still, he vowed to prove to her he could be mature in spite of the noticeable bulge below his belt buckle. In an effort to calm down, he ran through a mental laundry list of a few times he'd been in pain. His first broken rib during one rodeo. When Maria made him eat spinach. The day Abby had him served with divorce papers.

That did it, or so he thought until he faced Georgie again. The T-shirt hit her well above the knee and hung off one shoulder. He could see the outline of her breasts and that's exactly where his gaze landed again, and his imagination kicked into overdrive.

"Austin."

He finally tore his attention away from her attributes and came in contact with her scowl. "What?"

She pointed two fingers at her eyes. "Up here."

"Sorry," he muttered, although in some ways he wasn't.

Georgie dropped down onto the bed and patted the space beside her. "Sit for a few minutes."

She really expected him to remain upright after their recent make-out session? Yeah, she did, and so would his stepmothers. With that in mind, he perched on the edge of the mattress, keeping a decent berth between them. "So what's on your mind?"

"Us," she said as she stretched the hem of the shirt to her knees. "Everything we've been through over the years."

He smiled. "We have been through quite a bit."

"And during all that time," she continued, "our friendship always meant the most to me."

Now he got it. She was about to deliver the "let's be friends" speech. "Yeah, we've always had a good friendship, and some really friendly foreplay in the bed of my truck."

She playfully slapped at his arm. "You know what I mean. I'm referring to all those instances when we were there for each other, like the time I made an A minus in Mr. Haverty's class."

"Oh, yeah. You nearly had a nervous breakdown over that one. What about the time you helped me pass calculus?"

"And biology and world geography and, I believe, algebra one."

"You never had to help me with athletics."

"True enough."

They paused to share a smile before Austin said, "Now that we've established we've been friends for a long, long time, is there another point to this conversation?"

She studied her hands and twisted the silver ring round and round her little finger. "That's what I want from you right now, Austin. That's what I need from you."

Damn. "Fine. You've got it."

She leveled her gaze on his. "Problem is, I'm not sure you're capable of being only my friend."

Anger sent him off the bed to face her. "You're being freakin' unfair, Georgie. We were friends long before we were lovers."

"I just don't know if you're willing to go back to that. I'm not sure you can."

He might be willing, but that didn't take away the wanting. "I damn sure could be only your friend, and I'll prove it."

"How do you propose to do that?"

Hell if he knew. "From now on, when I see you, I'll only shake your hand."

That earned him her smirk. "If you say so."

"I say so." Starting now. He stuck out his hand. "Hope you sleep well."

Ignoring the gesture, she rose from the bed and damned if she didn't draw him into a hug. She then stepped back and smiled. "See there? You managed to accept a friendly show of affection and you didn't even try to cop a feel. Maybe I've underestimated you."

Yeah, she had, because it had taken all his fortitude not to grab her up and toss her back onto the bed. "I'm a lot stronger than you think, Georgie."

"Only time will tell, Austin. And I hope you get a good night's sleep, too."

"Not hardly," he muttered as he headed out the door and down the hall.

Being only friends with Georgia May Romero could be the biggest mountain he'd ever had to climb, but he was determined to do it. He would find some way to show her he could be the man she wanted him to be, even if it might do him in during the process.

To postpone the inevitable test of his mettle, he hoped that when he woke up in the morning, he'd find her gone.

Five

Before she went home, Georgie sought out an energy boost and the means to wake up after a restless night. She padded into the deserted upscale kitchen on bare feet, wearing Austin's oversize T-shirt and suffering from a mild hangover. She retrieved a cup from the gray cabinet and located the canister of dark roast on the white-quartz countertop, right next to the fancy coffeemaker that looked as if it might require a barista degree to operate it.

After two attempts, she finally figured out the formula and waited for the stainless carafe to fill before she poured the brew into the mug. Normally she preferred cream and sugar, but black coffee seemed more appropriate under the circumstance.

She leaned back against the center island, clutching the cup and worrying over her behavior after stupidly finishing off two high-powered cocktails the night before. But she couldn't blame her complete lack of control on the booze. Not when the situation involved a sexy cowboy.

How could Austin still affect her so strongly? How could she forget how he'd flitted in and out of her life without a second thought? More important, how could she disregard that he'd fathered her child and still didn't know it?

She had to tell him soon. When and where remained a mystery yet to be solved.

"Mornin'."

Georgie glanced to her right to see Austin trudging into the room, his hair slightly damp and his jaw blanketed with whiskers. He hadn't bothered to put on a shirt, but at least he'd had the wherewithal to put on a pair of faded jeans that rested a little too low on his hips to be deemed decent. She didn't need to see the slight shading of hair centered into his broad chest or the flat plane of his belly or that other stream of hair that disappeared into his waistband. She definitely didn't need to look any longer, but she did.

Bad Georgie. Bad, bad Georgie.

Austin seemed oblivious to her blatant perusal of his body and continued toward the coffeemaker to pour a cup. He briefly brushed against her shoulder and gave her a good whiff of manly soap as he turned to face her. "I thought you'd be gone by now, or at least dressed." He topped off the comment by raking his gaze down her body and back up again, slowly.

She experienced a sensual electric shock down to the bottom of her soles. "I just needed to wake up a bit before I drove. I'll be leaving very soon."

He sent her a sleepy grin. "Don't go on my account, unless you have appointments."

She took a sip of coffee before setting the cup on the counter. "Only emergencies on Saturday and so far I haven't had any."

"I could always put you to work in the barn."

He could do a lot to her in the barn that had more to do with pleasure. He already had. "I still have some boxes I need to unpack and some things to put away. I didn't have a lot of time to do that in the past two weeks since I dove right into work."

"Do you need help?"

If he stepped through her doorway, she'd be too distracted to get anything done. Not to mention he would notice all the signs pointing to a child in residence. "I'll manage, and I really need to get out of here."

Austin leaned a hip against the counter. "Before you leave, I have a proposition."

Oh, brother. "I believe we established there would be no more of that last night."

He looked highly incensed. "It's not *that* kind of proposition. I'm talking about my second favorite pastime—a trail ride on open land. Just you and me and total freedom."

She didn't dare ask about his first favorite pastime, although she suspected it was a toss-up between calf-roping and carnal endeavors. "Does that include prancing naked on the prairie?"

He released a low, sexy laugh. "No prancing on my end, and since it's going to be in the forties, naked won't be happening for the sake of my dignity."

Georgie suddenly longed for summer. "It's been a while since I've ridden for pleasure." When he smirked and opened his mouth to speak, she pointed at him. "Before you make some suggestive comment, I'm referring to horseback riding."

"I didn't have one dirty thought rolling around in my brain."

"Yeah, sure."

He winked and smiled. "Just so you know, it's been a while since I've ridden just for the heck of it. We could have a good time. As friends."

The friend part still concerned her. "When do you propose we take this ride?"

He forked a hand through his dark hair. "We'd leave out this afternoon and come back tomorrow."

She raised both hands, palms forward. "Wait a minute. You're talking about an overnight trip?"

"Yeah. We're gearing up for the opening of Texas

Extreme, so I thought I'd map out the best course for the trail ride for beginners."

"You can't do that in an afternoon?"

"We're going to be taking the guests on an old-fashioned campout, complete with a chuck wagon. We might even herd a few cows."

As much as Georgie would enjoy the getaway, warning bells rang out in her head. "Couldn't you ask Dallas to go with you?"

"Nope. Dallas is freaking out over the baby coming in less than a month. He barely leaves Paris's side."

That made sense, but still… "What about Houston or Worth?"

"Houston's busy chasing the dream and Worth, well, he's busy chasing women."

She was down to her last option. "That still leaves Tyler."

"He left this morning to check out a couple more pack mules for the trail ride and I'm not sure when he'll be back."

Georgie narrowed her eyes. "If you expect me to ride a mule, my answer is definitely no."

His grin arrived, slow as sunrise. "Do you have a problem with my ass?"

She slapped at his arm. "You're so comical this morning."

"Thanks, and for the record, I don't expect you to board a mule."

"Good to know, but my mare isn't ready for a trail ride. She's still pretty skittish."

"I know," he said. "I saw her dump you on your butt last week, remember?"

She wished she could forget. "I guess that settles it then. I don't have an adequate ride, so you're on your own."

"I still have the dynamic duo."

She was blasted back into the past to a wonderful time when they'd set out on horseback in secret. "You mean Junior and Bubba?"

"Yep. They're still going strong at the ripe old age of fifteen."

"I loved Junior."

"He probably feels the same about you. Only one way to find out. Come with me on the ride."

She turned the idea over and over and couldn't quite pull the trigger on a definitive decision. "I'm still not too keen on the overnight idea."

He rubbed a hand over his jaw. "Tell you what. If you agree to go, and you decide you don't want to spend the night with me, we'll ride back."

That she could live with, but she still had responsibilities. "I'll see what I can get done before noon and I'll let you know."

"Fair enough," he said. "But don't take too long. I want to get started right after lunch."

"If I do agree, what do you propose we have for

dinner? Or do you plan to play hunter and gatherer and catch our meal in the creek?"

He winked. "Leave that up to me. I promise you won't be disappointed."

He'd never disappointed her when it had come to showing her a good time. He *had* let her down during those two mornings when he'd disappeared out of her life to pursue his interests. Yet Chance had become the most important person in her life, and maybe this journey would present a prime opportunity to have a heart-to-heart with Austin.

On that thought, Georgie walked to the sink, rinsed out her cup then turned to find Austin staring at her. "Where and when do you want me to meet you?"

He looked mildly surprised. "Around one p.m., at the main barn. Be sure to bring a coat. The temperature's going to be dropping this afternoon when the cold front comes in."

She might be better served by wearing several layers of clothing for protection, both from the elements and her escort. "Okay. Right now I better get dressed and retrieve my truck."

He hooked a thumb behind him. "Your truck's in the driveway. Feel free to wear my T-shirt home."

Oh, sure. "With my high heels?"

He streaked a palm over his face. "Get out of here, Georgie, before I…"

She couldn't hold back a smile. "Before what?"

"Before I forget we're just friends."

Georgie needed to remember the friend pact, too, no matter what Austin Calloway might throw at her. But if their past behavior predicted future deeds, that would darn sure prove to be difficult.

"Where in the hell are you going?"

Austin ignored Dallas's question and continued to secure the bedrolls to Bubba's saddle. "I'm going to chart out the trail ride for Extreme."

Worth wandered into the barn and eyed the bay gelding. "Seems a little early to be worrying about that. The lodge isn't going to be finished for a couple of months and we haven't even started building the new catch pens yet."

Austin moved across the aisle to Junior and tightened the jet-black gelding's girth strap. "I'll be busy with the dealerships after the first of the year. I figure now's as good a time as any."

Tyler suddenly made an appearance to add to the unwelcome audience. "Since you have two horses saddled, I'm guessing you want one of us to go with you."

He began to shorten the stirrups without looking back. "Nope."

"You're going to take both horses?" Dallas asked.

Austin finished and finally turned around. "Yep."

Worth pulled a piece of straw from his pocket and

started chewing on it. "You must be planning to cross the border if you're taking both horses."

He really wished they'd all leave before Georgie arrived. The odds of that happening were slim to none, he realized, after he heard the sound of approaching footsteps. Austin braced for the fallout until Jenny—not Georgie—breezed into the barn, wearing a crazy red Christmas sweater and matching slacks.

She strode over and offered him a small square blue cooler and a plastic sack. "Here you go, sugar."

Austin took the containers, strode to Bubba and draped the straps over the saddle horn. "I appreciate it, Jen. Hope you didn't go to too much trouble."

When he faced Jenny again, she patted his cheek. "No trouble at all. Oh, and I just talked to Georgie. She said she had to make a phone call and then she'll be heading this way. Ten minutes tops."

Damn. The companion cat was out of the bag, and no doubt he'd have hell to pay. "Thanks for letting me know."

The look Dallas sent him wasn't lost on Austin. "Georgie, huh?"

He figured he should just fake indifference and hope for the best. "Yeah, Georgie. She wasn't busy this afternoon so we decided to do it together."

Worth chuckled. "Doing it together is a lot more fun than doing it alone."

Jenny sent her son a frown. "Hush, Worth Calloway. A man can go for a ride with a woman without anything disreputable going on." She turned her attention back to Austin. "Your supper should be set. I put in all the fixings for a wiener roast."

When the boys began to chuckle, Austin balled his fists at his sides, itching to throw a punch. Jenny's weapon of choice involved a stern look aimed at the brothers before she turned to him again. "I added marshmallows and I wasn't sure what Georgie liked on her hot dog, so just to be safe, I included several condiments."

"If you're really worried about safety, Mom," Worth began, "you might want to pack some condoms with the condiments."

Jenny laid a dramatic hand over her heart. "My dear, sweet child, don't be so crass. You're acting like an oversexed heathen."

Like a bunch of junior high jocks, the brothers' chuckles turned into full-fledged laughter. "Come on, guys," Austin said. "Get your minds out of the sewer and have some respect for Jen."

Jenny propped her hands on her hips. "Austin is absolutely right. You boys have apparently forgotten your raising."

"Sorry, Mom," Worth muttered, followed by Dallas's and Tyler's apologies.

Jenny gave Austin a quick hug. "I'll see you tomorrow, and, you two, be careful."

"We will," Austin said. "And thanks again for everything."

After Jen strode out of the barn, Tyler said, "I personally think Worth had a good idea about the condoms. Do you have one in your wallet that's not from your high school years?"

Austin had about enough. "Look, Georgie is just a friend. That's all. We're not doing anything we haven't been doing for years."

Dallas took on a serious expression. "That's what worries me. I've already warned you about—"

"Dammit, I know, Dallas." Austin drew in a calming breath and let it out slowly. "You're just going to have to trust me on this one. We're not the same stupid kids we used to be."

Tyler came up and slapped Austin on the back. "Good luck, bud. Wide-open spaces and a beautiful woman can equal a lack of control. If you can resist her, you're a better man than me."

"Or crazy," Worth added. "But if you only want to be friends with her, I'll be glad to pick up where you leave off."

Austin sent him a menacing glare. "Not every woman is interested in you, Worth."

Dallas stepped forward. "We're not trying to get into your business. We just don't want you leading Georgie on."

Same song, fiftieth verse. Austin understood where his brothers were coming from, but he was up for the challenge. He could have a platonic relationship with a woman, even one he'd slept with before. Even one he'd wanted to sleep with last night, minus the sleeping…

"Sorry I'm late."

His focus went straight to Georgie strolling down the aisle, her hair pulled up high into a ponytail. She wore a heavy flannel shirt over a white T-shirt, a pair of faded jeans and worn brown boots. With every move she made, every smile she gave the boys who now stood, hats in hands, staring at her, Austin's confidence began to slide.

He cleared the uncomfortable hitch from his throat. "No problem. I'm just now finishing up with the supplies."

She held up the small nylon duffel. "Do you have room for this?"

"What's in it?"

She glanced over her shoulder at the brothers, who continued to stand there like statues, eavesdropping. "Just a few essentials in case we lay over. Tooth-brush, toothpaste, that sort of thing."

Too bad she hadn't said a sexy nightgown, but he supposed that wouldn't be practical. Fantastic, yeah, practical, no. "Hang it over the saddle horn."

"Good idea." After she complied, she brought her attention to the brothers. "Are you guys going, too?"

Dallas shook his head. "Nope. I'm hanging out with the wife."

Tyler scowled. "I'm hanging out with the mothers."

"I'm hanging out at the local dance hall," Worth began, "but I'd be glad to change my plans and accompany you."

Georgie smiled at him sweetly. "I wouldn't feel right leaving all those local women without a dance partner."

Worth returned her smile. "You and me, we could take a stroll in the moonlight while Austin roasts a few marshmallows."

Austin pointed at the door. "Out. Now. All of you."

While the crew trudged away, Tyler muttered, "Fifty dollars says he'll need the condiments."

"I'll see your bet and raise you fifty," Worth added as they walked out the barn, laughing all the way.

Georgie frowned. "What was that all about?"

He checked to see if both bedrolls were secure beneath the saddles' cantles. "Nothing. They're just mouthing off like usual."

"It sounded like they were making some kind of bet on me."

Austin ventured at glance at Georgie to find she looked a little put out. "It has more to do with me. I told them this was a friendly trip, and they don't believe I can be only friends with you without getting too friendly."

"Can you?"

He was going to do his best. "Sure. Are you ready to roll?"

"I guess so."

He sensed her hesitation, and felt the need to reassure her. "Georgie, I promise to be a gentleman, just like Maria taught me to be. And if I slip up, Junior knows his way back to the barn."

She patted the black gelding's neck and received a nuzzle in return. "Yes, he does, and he's still as gorgeous as ever."

So was she. "Yep, he's in good shape. He also recognizes you."

She pulled the headstall from the hanger and began to remove the horse's halter. "We all had some unforgettable times."

Austin recalled one great time that had occurred not so far away in the tack room. Some hot and heavy kisses, taboo touches and a moment when they'd almost gone all the way. His focus went straight to her body and it took all his strength not to grab her up and carry her back in the cramped room to refresh her memory. "Are you ready to go?"

She sent him a look over her shoulder. "Do you plan to ride Bubba without a bit?"

Keep your mind on your business and not her butt, Calloway. "I probably could, but I guess it's best I don't."

After they were all tacked up, Georgie mounted Junior with ease and Austin followed suit on Bubba.

"Let's get this adventure started," he said as he guided the gelding down the aisle with Georgie and Junior tagging along behind them.

Once they emerged into daylight, they rode through the gate, side by side, and into open pastureland. A strong gust of wind kicked up some dust, and Austin wondered if Georgie had on enough clothes to keep warm. He could keep her warm. Give her his heat in ways she wouldn't forget…

"I've forgotten how wonderful this feels," she said, interrupting his suspect train of thought.

"Yeah. Nothing better than wide-open spaces." *Wide-open spaces and a beautiful woman can equal a lack of control.* Austin erased Tyler's warnings from his mind as they continued down the path leading to the creek.

They rode in silence for a long time before Georgie spoke again. "Any ideas on your route?"

He had some ideas, but none having to do with routes. "I thought I'd follow along the fence line for a couple of miles."

She sent him a fast glance. "That means you'll be bordering the road leading to my dad's ranch. Nothing will ruin an Old West fantasy more than a delivery truck."

He couldn't argue that point. "Hadn't thought about that. Then I guess we'll head south and ride toward the far end of the creek."

She looked straight ahead and smiled. "Ah, the

creek. I can remember spending a lot of summers at the place."

So could he. "The rope is still there, but the water isn't as deep as it used to be. I wouldn't suggest using it."

That earned him a sour look. "It's a little too cool to be swimming today, don't you think?"

He adjusted his hat on his head with one hand. "Probably so."

She favored him with a smile right out of a dirty dream. "Wanna race?"

He wanted to pull her off the horse and into his arms. He wanted her. Real bad. "No need to ask me twice."

He cued Bubba into a lope and Georgie didn't miss a beat. When he picked up speed, so did she, smiling all the way. And she became that girl again, the one who'd spurred his adolescent fantasies. A more mature version, but still as pretty. Still as spirited.

They ran headlong past the places where they used to meet in secret, sometimes at midnight, sometimes in broad daylight if they were feeling more daring, avoiding detection by their fathers and caught up in the thrill of trying not to get caught. They'd engaged in long conversations, when they hadn't been engaging in experimentation.

So many ghosts on this land. Good times mixed with the not so good. Most had been good, except for one in particular, the old windmill on the horizon serving as a reminder. The place where he'd planned to tell her goodbye before he'd left for college, but she hadn't shown up.

As they slowed their pace, Georgie's laughter echoed over the plains and, in that moment, he couldn't want her more. But he had to remember the friendship pact, and adhere to it. He had to take hold of some serious honor and not act on his desires.

If he could manage that accomplishment, then he expected to encounter a few flying pigs before the end of the day.

Six

Before the end of this trip, Georgie planned to fully disclose her secret to Austin. If only she could find the appropriate place, appropriate time and, most important, the appropriate words. Right then those words escaped her.

As they neared the familiar creek, she noticed gray clouds gathering on the horizon, completely concealing the sun. They'd been riding for a little over two hours when she sensed now would be a good time to take a break and assess the weather.

"Let's stop for a while," Austin said before she could get the suggestion out of her mouth.

They trotted to the tree line and, after they dismounted, led the horses to the shallow brook for a drink. Austin then took the reins from her hands and guided the geldings to the pasture to turn them loose.

"Shouldn't we tie them up?" she asked as soon as he returned to her side.

"Nah. They'll hang around here and if they don't, they'll find their way back to the barn."

Great. "And that would leave us stranded in the middle of nowhere on foot."

Without responding, Austin put both pinkies in his mouth and blew out a loud whistle, bringing the equine boys back in record time. He grinned at Georgie as he patted the geldings' necks. "They don't have any intention of going anywhere without me."

Georgie had felt the same way about him at one point in time. "They've always been well trained."

Austin rummaged around one of the saddlebags, withdrew two carrot chunks, laid them in his flattened palms and offered them to Junior and Bubba. "They know who feeds them." He waved them away. "Now you two go back to the grass for a bit."

As if they understood every word, the geldings turned around and hurried back to the pasture to graze. "You missed your calling, Austin. You should've been a lion tamer in the circus."

"Maybe so. I pretty much grew up in a circus." He wandered over to the bank and sat down on a rock. "Come over here and take a load off."

"I've been sitting for almost two hours."

"Then suit yourself and stand."

In reality, her legs felt a little shaky from the long ride, but the thought of sitting next to him didn't help matters. Still, this could be an opportunity to open up the lines of communication before she lowered the baby boom.

Georgie strolled over to Austin, lowered down onto the dirt slope and hugged her knees to her chest. "Looks like it might rain."

"The forecast says tomorrow midday."

She sent him a sideways glance. "This is Texas and when Mother Nature comes for a visit, she doesn't always listen to meteorologists."

"True."

A brief span of silence passed before Georgie spoke again. "I'm still amazed at Bubba's and Junior's obedience. Way back when, they were both pretty wild, especially Junior."

"But he pretty much taught you how to rope."

"With a little assistance from you."

He sighed. "Yeah. It's hard to believe how long they've been in my life. But so have you."

Yes, she had. A very long time full of happiness and heartache. She snatched up a stick and began tracing random circles in the soil. "How long did you know your wife?"

"For a while," he said. "We ran into each other on the circuit on a regular basis during my rodeo years before we got hitched."

A possibility burned into Georgie's mind, and it wasn't good. She shifted slightly to gauge his reaction to the impending question. "Were you dating her when your dad passed away?"

He studied her for a moment before reality dawned in his expression. "If you're asking if we were together when I was with you, the answer is not only no, but hell no. I can't believe you'd even think such a thing."

"What did you expect, Austin? I found out you'd married her four months after that night."

He lowered his gaze to the ground. "I guess that's a reasonable assumption under normal circumstances, but it shouldn't be with us. Not with our history."

A lot of their history hadn't exactly been hearts and flowers, or complete honesty. "When I didn't hear from you after that last night we spent together, I assumed you'd moved on again. I just didn't know you'd moved on into a marriage."

"More like a huge mistake."

For some reason the declaration pleased her. "Surely it wasn't all bad."

He ventured a quick glance in her direction. "Not all of it. Not in the beginning. But sex alone can't sustain a relationship."

She cringed at the thought of him with another woman, even though she'd never had any real claim on him. "Did it ever occur to you that maybe you two should have tried living together before tying the knot?"

Austin sent her a cynical grin. "The whole wedding was spontaneous, and stupid. Too much beer and too much time on our hands and a Vegas chapel at our disposal."

At least that explained the hasty nuptials. "Never in a million years would I have believed you'd be a drunken Vegas wedding cliché, Austin."

"Well, believe it. I tried to make it work but Abby wasn't willing. In fact, to this day, I'm still not sure what I did."

"Maybe it wasn't what you did, but what you didn't do."

He frowned. "What do you mean?"

He was such a guy. "Were you attentive? Romantic? Did you tell her you loved her more than once in a blue moon?"

He almost looked ashamed. "None of the above, and I'm not sure we were in love. I mean, I cared about her, but I knew the marriage idea was wrong when I finally signed the divorce papers and I didn't feel anything but relief."

"Yet you hung in there for quite some time, right?"

"Three years, but it was pretty much over in the first six months."

"Wow. I'm surprised you didn't end it sooner."

"I didn't want to admit to the failure."

Nothing new there. "You can't shoulder that burden alone. It takes two to make or break a solid marriage."

"Maybe you're right, but there was one thing she wanted that I wasn't willing to give her."

"What was that?"

"A kid. I told her several times I didn't want any, but she started making noise about two months into the marriage. I reminded her that wasn't in my immediate future."

His assertions gave Georgie pause. "Then you're not completely ruling it out."

He shrugged. "I'm not sure. I only know I'm not going to be ready for that responsibility for a long, long time."

Georgie swallowed hard around the swell of disappointment mixed with panic. She had to acknowledge one serious reality—Austin might never accept their son. "I guess I always saw you as the fatherly type. You did a good job keeping your younger brothers on the straight and narrow."

He picked up a pebble and tossed it into the creek. "But if they screwed up, it was ultimately my folks' responsibility. And maybe I got my belly full keeping them in line while my dad was off doing whatever he was doing aside from work."

Meaning marrying another woman and birthing two more boys without telling anyone. Essentially she had done something similar by not telling him about their child, although her reasoning had seemed honorable at the time. "Did his deception influence your attitude about having children at all?"

"Nah. That would be Dallas, although he obviously changed his mind." He stared off into space for a moment before presenting a surprising smile. "Do you think it's still here?"

He'd always been a master at changing the subject when it got too hot in the emotion kitchen. Admittedly she could use a break, too. "What is still here?"

"The tree."

She'd known it was still around from the moment they'd ridden up to the creek. "To my right, about three oaks down."

He slapped his palms on his thighs and stood. "Let's go look at it before we head out."

"Why?"

He took her hand and pulled her to her feet. "I could use a good memory about now."

Georgie had to admit that secret meeting site did hold more than a few fond recollections. "Oh, all right. Lead the way."

She followed behind Austin along the bank, weaving in and out of foliage, until they reached the memorial tree sporting a pair of initials. She ran her palm over the carvings. "I wonder if anyone ever saw this."

Austin came to her side and grinned. "If they did, I'm sure they're still trying to figure out the identity of R and J."

She returned his smile. "Randy and Jill?"

"Ralph and Julie."

"Ronald and Jessie."

"Wasn't that a real couple from high school?" he asked.

"Possibly, but I guarantee we didn't know any Romeos or Juliets." And that had been the inside joke—star-crossed lovers caught between feuding fathers. She turned and leaned back against the trunk. "At least no one packed any daggers or poison."

He braced his palm on the tree, right above her head. "But the first time I kissed you here, that really packed a punch."

A kiss that had almost sent her to her knees. "I suppose."

"Suppose?" He leaned forward and ran a fingertip along her jaw. "Maybe I should refresh your memory."

As he leaned forward and rested his other hand on her waist, Georgie fought that same old magnetic pull. She decided to verbally push back. "Why do you continue to do this?"

"Do what?"

"Test my strength."

He traced her lips with a fingertip. "Maybe I'm testing mine."

"Friends, Austin," she muttered without much conviction.

"Good friends, Georgie girl."

When Austin traced the shell of her ear with his tongue, Georgie released a ragged breath and shivered. And when he centered his gaze on her eyes, she tried to prepare for what would predictably come next…a kiss that she couldn't resist.

Then he stepped back and winked. "Guess I'm stronger than we both thought."

Georgie gritted her teeth and spoke through them. "You're a tease."

To the sound of Austin's laughter, she stormed away through the trees, half tempted to ride back in the direction of the ranch. She then realized she had no horse, and whistled at the geldings the way Austin had. They didn't budge, at least not for her. After Austin summoned them, they came running back, looking for a handout from their master.

Georgie didn't afford Austin a glance, didn't say a word, as they mounted their respective horses. Frustration kept her and Junior in the same spot as Austin headed away, leaving her behind. Frustration over his actions, and her typical feminine response.

A few moments passed before he glanced back and pulled Bubba to a stop, then turned the gelding to face her. "Do you have a problem?"

"Yes. You."

He released a low, grainy laugh. "Obviously you traded in your sense of humor to get that vet degree."

"I don't exactly find your determination to play with me very funny."

"Sweetheart, if I'd seriously played with you, you'd be moaning, not complaining."

Now why did that make her want to twitch in the saddle? "Look, before I agree to continue this little trip, you have to promise you won't tease me again."

He narrowed his eyes and studied her straight on. "Best I recall, you used to like to be teased, especially when I had my hand in your—"

"Austin," she cautioned, despite the damp heat gathering between her thighs.

He raised both hands, as if surrendering. "Okay. I'm sorry. Old habits die hard."

Old memories clearly never died. "Apology accepted, as long as you don't pull anything like that again."

"Okay. But keeping my hands off you isn't going to be easy. Keeping my mouth off you is going to be really tough."

A very detailed sexual image filtered into Georgie's mind, bringing about a blanket of goose bumps. The girl she'd once been might have begged him to end her misery, but she wasn't that girl anymore. She was a woman. A vital woman who hadn't been with a man in six years. A woman who desperately needed his touch, his kisses, but recognized that the cost of intimacy with this man could be too high. "Where are we heading now?"

"The old cabin."

Just one more monument to the past, she thought

as she cued Junior forward. She'd been at the ramshackle cabin before, but not to fool around with Austin. She'd met him there on his late mother's birthday at his request, an unusual appeal, but he'd been uncharacteristically sentimental. Those moments hadn't been about teenage hormones and unbridled lust. They'd been about comfort and communication. Buried regrets and obvious pain. Emotional exposure. Friendship at its finest.

Yes, she had been at that cabin, and during that fateful encounter, Georgie had quietly, completely fallen in love with Austin Calloway. Sadly, she still was, proving some things never changed.

The place hadn't changed a bit. Austin realized that when they arrived at the rickety structure that had somehow weathered at least a hundred years' worth of Texas heat. The windows were still boarded up, and he found that funny considering anyone could probably knock the door open with the swing of a rope. But his dad had always been a stickler when it came to security, even if it involved a one-room house that was barely hanging on. At least the front porch still appeared to be intact, and that might be a good thing if it rained.

He looked to his left to find Georgie staring at the cabin like she'd never seen it before. "It's exactly how I remembered it," she finally said. "Old and probably moldy."

Austin climbed off the saddle and guided Bubba to the pole barn adjacent to the cabin. "I imagine it's pretty dusty inside. Maybe even a critter or two hanging out."

Georgie dismounted and joined him. "Lovely. Nothing like stumbling upon a skunk."

"Skunks come out in the spring. Same with snakes. In fact, most of the animals are hibernating. Come to think of it, the last time I was here, I didn't see one living creature except maybe a spider or two."

"Bugs don't hibernate."

"That's true, but I don't see any reason why we'd have to go inside."

She studied the dreary sky. "A storm comes to mind."

"We'll worry about that if it happens." He needed to ask a question before they settled in for dinner. "Do you want to go back to the ranch?"

She sighed. "After sitting for the better part of six hours, I'd rather just relax for a while. We'll play the overnight plan by ear."

He couldn't deny his disappointment if she didn't spend the night with him, not that he expected anything to come of it aside from companionship. But that was okay. It was high time he relearned how to be her friend, although he figured he'd be fumbling his way through it. He also envisioned sitting on his hands and keeping his mouth shut when he wasn't talking. "All right then," he said. "Let's get these guys unsaddled. I'll turn them out with some hay, then I'll build a fire for dinner."

After they'd accomplished that goal, Austin retrieved the supplies, tossed them onto the porch and searched the yard for a few rocks to fashion a makeshift fire ring. He placed them in a circle in front of the house then went about gathering kindling from fallen limbs on the side of the house. He returned to find Georgie sitting on the top porch step, elbows resting on her knees, palms supporting her jaw, a smile on her pretty face.

He dropped the wood into the middle of the circle and faced her. "You look amused."

"You look cute, all dressed in your red flannel shirt, getting ready to cook dinner. A cross between Paul Bunyan and Betty Crocker."

"I'm not sure how I feel about that description."

She straightened and pushed her hair back from her shoulders. "I didn't mean to insult your manhood. Actually, I'm impressed you're going to be playing chef tonight."

"Don't be too impressed." He leaned over and pulled two of the straightest limbs from the pile. "Here's our utensils."

She laughed. "We're having hot dogs?"

"Yep."

"Darn. I was hoping for filet mignon."

"Sorry to disappoint you."

"I'm not disappointed at all, Austin. I'm looking forward to it because I'm starving. So come on, baby, light that fire."

He'd like to have his fire lit by her. Ignoring the dirty thoughts, Austin pulled an old book of matches from his back pocket. "Keep your fingers crossed this doesn't take more than a few tries. I don't have too many of these things."

Georgie came to her feet and brushed off her bottom. "We can always rub two sticks together."

Why the hell did hearing the word *rub* suddenly threaten his dignity? "Yeah, sure. You get going on that."

Turning his attention back to the fire pit, Austin struck the first match and watched it fizzle out. The second try didn't turn out any better. Now down to his last two, he wondered if they might have to return to the ranch for a decent meal. If that happened, he'd be sorely disappointed.

"Look what I found, Calloway."

Austin turned toward the porch where Georgie stood, holding a red-and-black barbecue lighter. "Where did you find that?"

She hooked a thumb over her shoulder. "In the sack back there. I also found marshmallows and a lot of little packets of condiments."

That reminded him of the previous condiment and condom conversation with the brothers. Funny thing was, he always carried a condom with him. Not that he had a snowball's chance in the desert to use it this trip. "That's Jenny for you. She hoards those things."

"They do come in handy."

After Georgie sprinted down the steps and gave him the lighter, Austin had little trouble getting the fire going, in spite of the steady breeze. Seated on the ground, they ate their hot dogs, roasted marshmallows, reminisced and laughed a lot. The whole time Austin kept his attention on Georgie's mouth, imagining another kiss. Imagining was all he could do, unless she gave him some sign she wanted it, too. Not a whole lot of chance that would happen.

By the time they were done with dinner, the only light that illuminated the area came from the dwindling fire. Austin found more wood to stoke the blaze, then returned to the porch to retrieve the one thing that would give him an excuse to have her in his arms. He set the radio on the wooden slats and tuned in to a country music station.

"Oh, my gosh," Georgie said from behind him. "You still have that relic?"

He turned to find she was real close. "Yeah, and it still works."

"If I'd known you wanted music, I would've brought my MP3 player and speakers."

He reached over and tucked one side of her hair behind her ear, revealing a pair of diamond heart studs. They looked a lot like the same earrings he'd given her for her sixteenth birthday. He'd worked overtime at the feed store to earn enough money to buy them for her, and it had been worth it when she'd been so damned pleased. "I enjoy having the past around now and then."

She smiled. "So do I."

On cue, the radio went from a commercial break to a country ballad. "Care to dance with me again?"

"Twice in one week? That's so daring."

And kind of dangerous if he didn't control his hands and mouth. "You've never shied away from risky behavior."

"That was before…" Both her gaze and words trailed off.

"Before what?"

"Before I became an adult with adult responsibilities. However, I wouldn't refuse a dance with the consummate cowboy."

"Good to know."

After taking Georgie's hand, he led her down the steps and close to the fire where he put his arms around her. She laid her head on his shoulder and he placed his palm lightly against her back. As the song continued, he found his hand drifting lower, like he didn't have control of his appendages. He managed to stop the progress before he lost the wager that he could ignore his libido. But if she made one encouraging move, all bets were off.

They remained that way for a time as the wind picked up steam, and then came the deluge. Georgie

pulled back and did something Austin would have
never predicted. She laughed. Just the sound of it
caused him to laugh, too. They continued to stand
there, drenched to the bone and behaving like pre-
schoolers who didn't have the good sense to come
out of the rain.

When he noticed she was shivering, he led her to
the porch, drew her against him and held her close.
Then she did something else he didn't expect—
brushed her lips across his neck.

He bent his head and took her mouth with a ven-
geance, sliding his tongue against hers slowly, de-
liberately, and she responded with a little action of
her own. They stayed that way through one more
song, making out like they had as kids. But the man
in him backed her against the wooden wall, grabbed
her butt and pressed against her, seeking relief but
finding none. And what he was about to do wouldn't
help a damn bit, but he wanted to do it. Had to do it.

He shoved her shirt off one shoulder then slid the
strap to the tank she wore underneath down her arm
partway. Now that he'd gained access, he broke away
and took her breast into his mouth, circling her nipple
with the tip of his tongue. She answered by undress-
ing enough to reveal her other breast and framed his
head in her hands. The small sexual sound she made
drove him to the brink of insanity, pushed him toward forbidden territory. Right then, right there, he
could take her down to the ground just to be inside

her. Instead, he decided he would make this about her, but only if she agreed.

With that goal in mind, Austin released the button on her jeans and paused for a protest. When that didn't happen, he slid the zipper down and whispered, "Do you want me to stop?"

"I…" She let out a long, broken breath. "No. Don't stop."

That was all he needed to hear. He worked his hand into her jeans, where he rimmed the edge of her panties. She gave no indication she'd changed her mind, which drove him to keep going, keep searching beneath the silk for that very sweet spot. She was warm and wet and definitely ready for the attention. He gave it to her with slow strokes before he quickened the pace. She gripped his shoulders tightly, moved her hips rhythmically in time with his touch.

After she tensed, he raised his head from her breasts and brought his mouth to her ear. "It's okay, babe. Just let go."

And she did, with a rush of dampness and a low, ragged moan. He didn't let up until he knew he had milked every last pulse of her climax and she collapsed against him. He kissed her again, softly this time, as he pulled her clothes back into place. He turned away and rested his palms on the railing to regain some scrap of composure.

"Austin, are you okay?"

As okay as he could be with a flaming erection and no place to go to douse it. "I'm fine."

"Well, I'm not."

He prepared for a lecture that no doubt would arrive soon, swift and sure. And since he'd gone back on his word, tossed the friendship pact to the wind, he damn sure deserved it.

Seven

Georgie truly wanted to scold him, but this wasn't all his fault. He had asked if she wanted to stop, and she'd told him no. She wasn't some weak wilting flower with no free will. Truth was, she had wanted him so much she hadn't been able to control the familiar underlying chemistry. They were combustible together. They always had been. She'd known that when she'd agreed to come with him. Deep down she knew this would likely happen. And in all honesty, she didn't care, even if she should.

She stood there, shivering, her damp shirt and jeans only adding to her overall discomfort. "I'm freezing."

He pushed away from the banister and faced her. "Understandable. You're soaked to the skin."

"So are you."

"Sweetheart, that's the least of my concerns at the moment."

She sent a pointed look at his distended fly, somewhat surprised that he didn't invite her to finish what they'd started.

"Take your clothes off, Georgie."

Apparently she'd been mistaken. "Excuse me?"

He bent over, snatched one of the blankets from the floor and tossed it to her. "Don't look so worried. I'm not going to ravish you."

"You just did."

His patent slow grin came out of hiding. "Yeah, I did, and I don't regret it because obviously you really needed it."

Boy, had she. "It's been a while."

"Same here."

She had a hard time believing that. "Try six years."

Shock passed over his expression. "You mean—"

"The last time you and I were together was the last time for me. Now turn around so I can get these clothes off."

He started unbuttoning his shirt. "I've seen you naked before."

"Maybe, but I'd rather that not happen now."

"Fine, but if I turn around, you're going to see my bare ass."

"Not if I don't look." Maybe she'd take just a little peek. Or a long gander.

"Alrighty then."

Georgie made quick work of shedding her clothes, socks and boots, while Austin took his sweet time. She was already wrapped securely in the blanket by the time he shoved down his pants. She remained glued in place, holding the blanket closed with one hand and her wet clothes in the other. She studied all the planes in his broad back, the buns of steel, the strong thighs and calves dusted with hair, and decided she couldn't speak if her life depended on it. Then he did something completely off-the-wall—laced his hands behind his neck and flexed his muscles, then did some crazy thrust reminiscent of a male-stripper movie she'd seen a while back.

A chuckle bubbled up in her throat and came out in a full-fledged laugh when he looked over one shoulder and grinned. "Stop it," she said when she'd recovered her voice. "And cover up."

"You didn't like my moves?"

Oh, yeah. "Please put something on before you catch a good case of pneumonia."

"Fine, but just let me know if you want some more cheap entertainment."

She averted her gaze when he leaned over and snatched the blanket from the porch slats. When she ventured another look, fortunately she found him covered from the waist down. Of course, that left his stellar chest in full view.

In order to distract herself, Georgie draped her shirt, jeans and pink panties over the railing while he came to her side to do the same. Once that was done, she faced him with a frown. "What now?"

"I guess we could go to bed."

"We don't have a bed."

"We have a couple more blankets and a dry floor in the cabin, unless you want to sleep out here."

A sudden clap of thunder and subsequent bolt of lightning told her that wouldn't be wise. "The cabin it is. Did you bring a flashlight?"

"Yep. It's in that bag behind you."

"Then get it."

"You're closer."

She muttered a few mild oaths as she bent down, opened the canvas duffel and rifled through the contents. "You brought clothes."

"An old shirt and a few rags. Keep going."

Of course the flashlight happened to be on the bottom. She straightened and handed it to him. "You're going in first."

"I wouldn't have it any other way."

Austin opened the door and shone the beam into the vacant cabin. Georgie followed him inside and couldn't see much of anything aside from the pine floor and barren walls, but she didn't spot any wildlife, either. Then suddenly he spun around and headed out the open door, leaving her all alone, in the dark.

"Austin Calloway, where are you going?"

"Don't panic," he said as he returned with the light. "I just grabbed the rest of the bedding so we can tolerate the bare floor."

"I'm not sure I'll get much sleep with the threat of vermin hanging over me."

"I'll protect you," he said. "Here, hold this so I can see what I'm doing."

She aimed the beam on her half-naked bed buddy while he spread out two more blankets, one on top of the other. Once that was done, he rolled what appeared to be the aged shirt and the aforementioned rags into two pillows.

"Your accommodations are ready, ma'am," he said.

"Not exactly a five-star hotel, but it will do."

Austin dropped down onto the pallet and patted the blanket. "Soft as a mattress."

"Maybe a concrete mattress." Georgie lowered herself beside him and scanned the room with the narrow beam, thankful she didn't see any animal eyes staring back at her.

"Hand it over, Georgie."

"Why?"

He stretched out on the pallet, easy as you please, not leaving a lot of space between them. "I don't want to wake up with a light shining in my eyes because you heard a noise. Worse still, I don't want you whacking me with it when you mistake me for a raccoon."

She reluctantly relinquished the flashlight and laid back, making sure the blanket was secure around her. Still, she didn't find much comfort in the limited covers, the floor beneath her or his close proximity. "I wonder how long this storm is going to last. If it doesn't end soon, our clothes won't be dry."

"You brought an extra pair of panties."

She paused until the shock subsided. "How do you know that?"

"I peeked inside your bag."

"That makes you a snoop, don't you think?"

"Yeah, you're right. Sorry. Sometimes I'm just a little curious."

A little too familiar with her, she decided, as she rolled to face him. "Extra panties or not, they're not going to do me much good when we head back to the ranch."

"You wouldn't be the first woman to ride naked as a jaybird through town on a horse."

"Very funny."

He turned the light on her. "I'd buy tickets to that, and so would every man in a thirty-mile radius."

She refused to honor him with a response. "Turn that thing off, please. I'm half-blind."

"You got it."

After he snapped off the flashlight, silence hung

over them for a few moments before he spoke again. "How many boyfriends have you had in the past six years?"

None. Zero. Nada. "There you go again, being intrusive."

"Hey, I told you about my marriage. Turnabout is fair play, right?"

He did have a point. "If you must know, I was too busy to date."

"You're saying you didn't have one man in your life?"

Only her little man. "No, I did not, and I assumed you would figure that out when I told you how long it's been since I've had sex. And for your information, women don't have to have a man to be happy. I had school and now I have my career, and that's all I need."

"All signs pointed to the contrary on the porch a little while ago."

Darn his insistence on reminding her of her vulnerability. "I had a moment of weakness."

"You had one hell of an orgasm. Do you want another one?"

Oh, yes… "No, thanks. That should last me another six years."

He chuckled. "Sweetheart, I don't believe for a minute that's true. And if it is, you're a lot stronger than me."

"I don't know about that. You didn't ask for a thing in return after our interlude."

"Interlude? Is that sophisticated talk for foreplay?"

"Go to sleep, Austin."

"Whatever you say, Georgie girl. And FYI, I apologize in advance for the tent I'll be pitching in the morning underneath this blanket."

That sent all sorts of naughty visions running amok in Georgie's mind. But the heat those fantasies generated did little to rid her of the sudden cold when a breeze blew through the ancient cabin. She pulled the blanket closer and tried hard to control her shivering body and chattering teeth, to no avail.

"Roll over, Georgie."

"I beg your pardon?"

"I'm going to put my arms around you because you're cold."

"We're also naked."

"All the better."

"No way."

"We'll keep the blankets between us."

She wanted to rebuff his request, but her chilled state wouldn't let her.

After Georgie shifted to her side, away from him, he scooted flush against her and wrapped her up in his strong arms. She had the strongest urge to rub her hands over that masculine terrain but realized it would be in her best interest to remain cocooned in the blanket, maintaining some semblance of separation. "Try to make sure we don't have any skin-to-skin contact."

"Darlin', we already have several times in the past."

"But this is the present. We don't need to stir up something again."

"Too late."

Infuriatingly sexy man. "Good night, Austin."

"Good night, sweetheart."

Georgie closed her eyes, but sleep wouldn't come. She thought about her schedule for the following week, a spattering of Monday appointments, lunch with Paris on Tuesday, her son's arrival home on Thursday.

Her son. *Their son.* She had very few hours to tell Austin the truth if she stuck to her original plan. She had so many qualms about doing that very thing after his previous statement about not wanting to be a father for a long time.

He *was* a father. But could he transition into being a dad to a little boy who needed one so desperately?

As soon as she finally confessed, only then would she know for sure. And that confession would need to come in twenty-four hours or less.

Austin woke up with an erection as hard as a hammer and a sexy woman beside him. He rolled to his side, bent his elbow and supported his jaw with his palm to do a little studying of that woman.

At some point during the night, Georgie had flipped onto her belly, the blanket draped low to expose her dark hair trailing down her back, her eyes closed tightly against the morning light. He took a visual trip down what he could see of her body and paused where he glimpsed the curve of her bottom.

He wanted to uncover her completely, make love to her until noon. Maybe even later. Then suddenly she caught him off guard when she shifted to her side and draped her arm over his bare hip underneath the covers. Worse still, she buried her face into his chest, right below his sternum, and he could feel the warmth of her lips pressed against his skin.

Oh, man, what was he going to do now? He knew what he'd like to do, but since he saw no real signs she was fully awake, he remained in the same position, rigid as an anvil. All of him.

Refusing to take advantage of a woman in a sleep-induced coma, Austin considered all the ways he could bring her around and a kiss came to mind. Or a touch. Or the sound of a honking horn outside the cabin.

Startled, Georgie popped up and looked around like she needed to gain her bearings. "What was that?"

Unfortunately for Austin, those thick locks of hair concealed her breasts. "I think someone's here."

"Who?"

"I'm not sure, but I'll find out." And he planned to give them a piece of what was left of his mind.

He came to his bare feet, taking the blanket with him and tucking it around his waist to hide the result of his sinful thoughts. He then strode to the window and swiped the dust from the panes to discover one familiar black truck and two equally familiar men leaned back against it. "It's Dallas and Houston."

"Oh, no. What are they doing here?"

"I have no idea, but I'm damn sure going to find out."

Austin swept open the door and closed it behind him after he stepped onto the porch. He immediately noticed his brothers eyeing the discarded clothes draped over the rail.

"Nice panties," Houston said. "I wouldn't have pegged you for a pink kind of guy."

He'd just stepped on his last nerve. "What in the hell do you two want?"

Dallas held up his hands. "Simmer down, Austin. We thought you might be needing a ride."

Likely story. "We've got two perfectly good geldings as transportation, so thanks but no thanks."

"Two geldings that showed up at the barn this morning," Houston added. "They must not have taken too kindly to the storm."

Damn. "Maybe we'll just walk back."

Dallas smirked. "You might want to ask Georgie if she's up for a six-mile hike."

Houston rubbed his stubbled chin. "Georgie, huh? Glad that explains the panties on the porch. I was worried about you, bro."

He didn't appreciate their kidding, or their laughter or the fact that they'd just shown up, unannounced. "You guys could've called. I have my cell with me."

Dallas exchanged a look with Houston before regarding Austin again. "Actually, Jen called and when she didn't get a hold of you, she called me to check on you two."

Austin realized he hadn't taken the phone from the bag, and he hadn't checked the battery. "Fine. Give us a few minutes and we'll head back with the two of you. And you better be on your best behavior around Georgie."

"Before you go inside," Houston said, "I have a question."

That was the last thing he needed, more stupid questions. "Make it quick."

"Could you not have waited until you got in the house before you started taking off your clothes?"

He'd had too little sleep and not enough sex to deal with this. "Not that it's any of your concern, but we both got wet."

Dallas chuckled. "I just bet you did."

Austin pointed at the truck. "Go start up the rig and we'll be out as soon as we're finished."

"Finished with what?" Houston asked, looking way too amused.

Austin ignored the question, grabbed all the clothes, both pairs of boots and headed into the cabin without looking back. "Get dressed," he said as he tossed Georgie her things. "The horses went back to the barn so Dallas and Houston are taking us back."

She shimmied her panties into place beneath the blanket, sparking Austin's fantasies. "I can only imagine how this looks to them," she said as she worked the tank top over her head, giving him a glimpse of her nipple. "I'm sure they think something wicked happened between us last night."

He'd like to try out a little wicked right now, to hell with his brothers. "They do think something happened, and actually, it did."

She sent him a harsh look as she put on both her shirts and then tossed the blanket back to wriggle into her jeans. "I prefer not to be reminded of my few moments of weakness."

He dropped the blanket without regard to his naked state. "Darlin', if it was that forgettable, then I'm not doing my job."

She stared below where his belt would be, then brought her gaze up to his eyes. "If you decide to return to the ranch like that, then we'll definitely be the talk of the D Bar C, if not the nearest town."

He grinned when he noticed her attention drifting downward again. "As soon as you're done looking, I'll put my pants on."

"I'm not looking," she said as she scrambled to her feet. "Now please get dressed."

"Yes, ma'am."

While Georgie pulled on her boots, Austin managed to get into his clothes in record time. He helped her gather the bedding and walked out the door to meet the verbal firing squad, thankful to find they were both seated in the truck's cab. After tossing the supplies into the bed of the truck, Austin opened the back door for Georgie and they climbed inside.

"Good to see you, Houston," she said in a meek voice. "How's it going on the circuit?"

"Good to see you, too, Georgie," he replied. "I'm doing fairly well so far this year."

When Austin draped his arm over the back of the seat, Georgie shifted closer to the door and asked, "How's Paris, Dallas?"

"She's cranky," he answered. "She told me to tell you she's looking forward to your lunch together in San Antonio on Tuesday."

Austin wouldn't be surprised if he ended up being the primary topic of conversation during that meeting. "You're off on Tuesday?"

She clutched her shirt closed, like she thought he might actually make a pass at her in the backseat. If they were alone, he would. "I don't have any appointments that afternoon, although everything is slowing down with the holidays fast approaching."

Austin hadn't experienced much of the Christmas

spirit in spite of the fact that he'd been surrounded by excessive decorations for the past few weeks. He hadn't bought any gifts, except for one, and he'd been saving that for the right time. That right time might not come until spring, at this rate.

All conversation died during the ride back, and after Dallas dropped them off in the driveway of his house, Austin turned to Georgie before she had a chance to climb into her truck and escape. "Do you want to come in and take a shower?"

After fishing the keys from her pocket, she tossed her bag into the passenger seat, closed the door and faced him. "First of all, I don't have any extra clothes aside from the damp ones I'm wearing. Second, I live only five minutes away. And lastly, I prefer to shower alone."

Not what he wanted to hear. He began his own countdown to counter hers. "First, I have a pair of sweats and a T-shirt you could wear. Second, you look cold and miserable and even five minutes will feel like five hours in those wet jeans. Third, I didn't say you had to shower with me, although I'm never opposed to saving water." When she just stood there, arms folded beneath her breasts, he decided to sweeten the deal. "I'll even cook you breakfast."

"You don't cook, Austin."

True that. "I can make scrambled eggs and bacon. I can have a pot of coffee on in a few minutes."

"Maybe some other time."

He really didn't have a clue as to why he was so desperate to keep her there. Why he couldn't just let her go and get on with his day? "Tell you what. Why don't you come here for lunch? It's Maria's turn to cook and she's most likely going to make her famous enchiladas."

She hesitated a moment before asking, "What time?"

"Usually around one."

"Okay."

That was way too easy. "You're going to accept, just like that."

"Yes. And afterward, we need to talk."

"About?"

"I'll see you at one, Austin."

He followed her as she rounded the hood and slid into the driver's side. "Can you give me a hint?" he asked before she closed the door on him.

"Sorry. You'll just have to wait until I'm clean and coherent."

Austin watched her drive away, wondering what he'd done this time that would warrant a serious conversation. He suspected it had to do with his continual pursuit of her affections. Maybe she'd decided she didn't want to be friends. Maybe she wanted nothing else to do with him.

He could drive himself crazy trying to figure it out, or he could go inside, shower and grab some coffee. After that, he'd distract himself with chores, and prepare for anything that might come out of Georgia May Romero's sweet mouth.

"Hello, baby boy."

"Hi, Mama."

Georgie held the phone tightly, wishing she was holding her son. "Are you having fun?"

"Uh-huh. We rode the rides and played some little golf and we even saw Santa and I got to ask him for presents!"

Georgie chuckled over the usage of "little" instead of "miniature" golf comment, but she didn't dare correct him. "That's great, sweetie. What did you tell him you wanted?"

"A fire truck and some games and a pony."

She'd been working on the last wish. "That's some list, Chance."

"I asked him for one more thing."

"What?"

"My daddy, but I don't think he can bring me him."

Her heart broke over the sadness in his voice, and cemented her goal to work on that, too, though she feared the outcome. "Tell you what, sweetie. When you get home, we're going to make cookies together and go pick out a real Christmas tree. How does that sound?"

"Okay, I guess. I gotta go. We're going to go see some sharks."

"That sounds wonderful, Chance. Now put your grandmother…"

The line went dead before her son could answer her request. She would call her mother later, when she returned from Austin's house, because that might be the time when she'd need her most.

On that thought, Georgie postponed the shower and opted to take care of the horses, all the while rehearsing what she would say to the father of her child.

Hey, Austin, guess what? You have a kid. Hey, Austin, a funny thing happened the last time we were together. I gave you comfort and you gave me a child. Hey, Austin, this little boy needs you, and so do I.

She truly didn't want to need him, but she did, and so did Chance.

After tending to the livestock, she returned to the house, bathed and laid across the bed to take a brief nap before the moment of truth arrived. She decided to be positive, let herself imagine they could live as one big, happy family. Let herself dream that Austin loved her, too, and he would love their son equally. That he would forgive her for waiting so long to tell him. Yet deep in her soul, she knew that would probably prove to be only a pipe dream.

Georgie soon drifted off into fitful sleep, and woke with a start when she realized she hadn't set an alarm. She glanced at the clock to discover the digital number displaying five past noon and shot out of the bed to get ready. She dried her hair, put on a little makeup, tried on three different outfits before settling on black slacks and a red silk button-down blouse covered by a black cardigan. She even chose to wear real shoes—a pair of simple black flats.

After putting on a pair of simple silver hoops, she ran a brush through her hair, took one last look in the mirror as well as a few deep breaths, then grabbed her keys, sent a text to Austin letting him know she was on her way and dropped the phone into her black purse.

On the way to the D Bar C, she said a little prayer, recited a few wishes, hoped for a miracle and grew more anxious as she approached the ranch's entrance. By the time she pulled into Austin's driveway, she was a twisted bundle of nerves.

She exited the truck, silently chanting, *It's time, it's time*, all the way to the front door. But when Austin greeted her wearing a black shirt and hat, crisp jeans and a winning smile, she wondered if she would be strong enough to say what she needed to say. He gestured her inside, then closed the door behind them, and as they stood there in silence, studying each other, the tension was palpable.

"Is something wrong?" she asked when he continued to stare.

"Lunch won't be ready for another hour. Something about Jen burning the tortillas."

"Oh. It happens. I guess we could go to the house and visit with everyone."

"Or we could stay here." Austin moved closer, searched her eyes and touched her cheek. "You are so damn beautiful."

She began to feel light-headed, vulnerable, fearful that she might not be strong enough to resist him. "You know what they say about beauty, Austin."

"It's in the eye of the beer holder?"

Did he have to be so darn cute? "Something like that."

"I'm not holding any beer. Besides, you're also smart, honest and sexy as hell."

She could certainly debate the honesty, considering what she'd been holding back. She also knew what would happen next if she didn't keep her wits about her. But common sense was no match for that continuous spark, or the sensual words the irresistible cowboy whispered in her ear, followed by a deep, provocative kiss.

"I need you, Georgie. I swear you've been all I've thought about since we met up again in the arena."

He'd never been far from her thoughts for years. "I need you, too, Austin, but if we keep giving in, where does that leave us?"

"As far as I'm concerned, we're two consenting adults who enjoy each other's company. We always have. I don't want to be only your friend, Georgie."

"What does that mean?"

"I want to spend time with you, out in the open, without worrying about what anyone thinks."

For years Georgie had longed to hear him say that, but she also recognized he might change his mind once he learned the truth. "Austin, there's something I need to say."

He pressed a fingertip against her lips to silence her. "We can talk later. Right now, I just want to be with you. I want *all* of you."

That *It's time* chant that had been running through Georgie's mind suddenly became *Later. Much later.* Maybe she was simply stalling. Maybe she'd grown weary of fighting the attraction. Maybe she just needed to be with the man she had always loved, perhaps for one final time. "Then, cowboy, take me away."

When Austin literally swept her off her feet and into his arms, Georgie surrendered to her needs, to this strong, handsome man, as she had so many times in the past. As she had last night, when he'd required nothing more than giving her pleasure. Now it was her turn to reciprocate.

Lunch, and the all-important talk, would simply have to wait.

Eight

Georgie closed her eyes as Austin carried her into his room and laid her across the bed. When she opened them, he pulled her up, removed her cardigan and paused with his hand on the top button of her blouse, indecision in his blue eyes.

"I want to make love to you, sweetheart, but only if you want it, too."

She swept one hand through her hair. "I do want it, even if I probably shouldn't."

"But—"

"Let's not talk it to death, okay?"

"That's all I needed to hear."

Everything happened in a rush then. She kicked

off her shoes, he toed out of his boots. He unbuttoned her blouse, she undid his shirt. Together they pulled off their pants, leaving them clad in only their underwear. Austin slowed down the pace when he removed her bra, then stood by the bed and shoved down his boxer briefs, leaving no doubt he was primed and ready. After he leaned over and slid her panties away, she expected him to join her, yet he surprised her by sending soft kisses down her torso.

Georgie knew where he was heading, and the thought made her hot as blazes and damp with anticipation.

He stopped below her navel and smiled up at her. "Remember the first time I did this?"

As if it had happened yesterday. "In my bedroom, right before you left for college."

He rubbed his knuckles along the inside of her legs, coaxing them apart. "I wasn't sure you trusted me enough, but you proved me wrong."

Funny, she'd trusted him enough to allow him to do anything, even when they were teens. "I admit I was a little scared, but it turned out to be one of the most memorable experiences I've ever had."

"One you want to repeat?"

"Yes," came out of her mouth in a breathy sigh.

After Austin bent her knees and moved between her legs, Georgie understood the futility in trying to talk. She struggled to stay still when he feathered kisses down the insides of both her thighs. She stifled a moan as he worked his way up and his mouth hit home. She involuntarily lifted her hips toward him, demonstrating how much she needed his attention, and where.

He knew exactly how to use his tongue in slow, deliberate strokes, driving her to the brink. He knew how to let up before she let go, then start again until the pressure began to build. He kept the pace for a few more moments, a sensual tug-of-war until she was prepared to lose the battle. And then he used the pull of his lips to completely shoot her over the edge into an orgasm so intense, she literally cried out.

Georgie clutched the sheet in her fists as she continued to ride the waves of the climax, only remotely aware that Austin had left the bed, and extremely aware when he returned, condom in hand. "Are we ready for this?" he asked as he held up the silver packet.

She glanced at his impressive erection. "You definitely are."

He tore into the package like a dog with a ham bone. "That I am."

Feeling a bit daring, and somewhat impatient, Georgie held out her hand. "Let me do it."

He favored her with a grin as he answered her request. "My pleasure."

"It will be."

And she made sure to focus on that pleasure when he fell back onto the bed. After tossing the condom aside, she swept her hair back with one hand and kissed her way down his belly, the same as he had done to her. She had a few tricks of her own, lessons learned from him, and put them in play, sliding her tongue down the length of him, then back up again.

"Damn, sweetheart," he muttered. "If you keep doing that, this is going to be one short ride."

"We can't have that," she said as she sat up, retrieved the condom and rolled it in place.

He clasped her arm and pulled her atop his chest. "Do we go traditional or your favorite position?"

She was both pleased and surprised he remembered. "What do you think?"

"Your favorite it is. Turn to your side."

Georgie rolled away from him and waited for that first sensation, that sense of completion. Luckily she didn't have to wait long as Austin draped her leg over his, then eased inside her. The last time she'd been in this position, little had she known they'd made a baby. He still didn't know, but he would in the near future.

All thoughts of sins and secrets faded away as Austin kissed her neck and placed his hand between her legs to again tenderly manipulate her.

"Austin, I don't think I can."

"You can. You will. I promise."

He made good on that vow in a matter of seconds with deep thrusts and deliberate caresses. She wanted so badly to see his face so she'd know when he reached his own climax, but her choice dictated that wasn't to be. She simply relied on the unsteady cadence of his breathing, the strength of his thrusts, the tension in his entire body and the one crude word that slipped out of his mouth.

Austin held her tightly then, his face buried in the back of her neck. She wanted to remain this way indefinitely. She wanted to shut out the world and the burden of truth, but that wasn't logical.

After Austin slid out of her body, Georgie shifted to face him. "It's probably past time for lunch."

He pressed his lips against her forehead. "I'm not that hungry right now."

She released a laugh. "Oh, come on, Austin. You're always starving after sex."

He gave her a slow grin. "Only when I'm finished having sex."

"You're kidding, right?"

"Nope. I have to have some time to recover, so I'm thinking we should put my big ol' shower to good use."

She liked that idea, but… "What about Maria and Jenny? They're not going to be happy if we don't make an appearance."

"I'll call them and tell them we got tied up." He gave her a quick kiss. "Better still, I'll send a text. That way, I won't have to explain anything in detail."

Thank goodness for small favors, and modern technology. "Good plan."

Austin grabbed his phone from the nightstand, typed in the message, then smiled. "First one in the shower gets to set the temperature."

Georgie was in the bathroom and standing at the shower before Austin even made it to the door. Unfortunately she could only stare at a panel of illuminated blue lights, completely perplexed. "How do you work this?"

Austin reached around her and pushed a button, then keyed in a number, sending several spray heads into action. "It's not rocket science."

She glanced back at him. "It's a little too high-tech for me. What happened to just turning a knob?"

He leaned over and kissed her neck. "If you really want to turn one—"

"I already have."

His rough, sexy laugh gave her more than a few pleasant chills. "Yes, ma'am, you sure did. And it was mighty fine."

Georgie yanked open the glass door and stepped inside the spa-like shower, decorated in brown stone and trimmed in copper mosaic, then attempted to avoid the overhead spray. "I don't want to get my hair wet," she said when Austin joined her.

Without regard to her wishes, Austin pulled her beneath the jet, soaking every inch of her.

She gave him a mock frown. "Not fair."

He kissed her softly, touched her gently, stoking

the fire again. "Everything's fair in love and water wars."

"Clever," she said as she reached for the shower gel clearly made for men. "Turn around and I'll wash your back."

"If I don't turn around, what will you wash?"

Cowboy cad. "Hold your horses, Calloway. I'll get to that."

"Lookin' forward to it."

Austin finally turned around, leaving Georgie with an up close view of his broad back and undeniably tight butt. She lathered her hands, then set out to search the terrain with her palms, taking her time investigating every plane, angle and dip at her disposal. Yet Austin disturbed her exploration when he turned around and grabbed the gel from the built-in soap dish.

"Wait a minute," she protested. "I'm not done yet."

He squeezed a few drops into his palm. "Yeah, you are, and I don't want you turning around."

"Interesting. I am going to smell like a guy."

His hands immediately went to her breasts. "You sure as hell don't look like one, and you don't feel like one, either."

No, she felt like a truly desirable woman. A naughty nymph. A needy female when the water play turned into more foreplay. The kisses were hot, the touches deliberate—both his and hers—and in a matter of moments, he had her in the throes of another strong climax. Then, before Georgie realized what was happening, Austin backed her against the tile, dangerously close to throwing caution out the window.

She braced her hands on his face to garner his attention. "Austin, we can't. We don't have any birth control."

He stepped back, went to her side and braced both hands on the wall. "Damn. I know better. Not once have I ever forgotten a condom."

"Yes, you did." And he was still ignorant of the outcome of that mistake.

He straightened and gave her a confused look before reality showed in his expression. "The last night we were together. We were damn lucky."

Oh, but they hadn't been, although despite the consequences, she wouldn't take anything for the time she'd spent with their child. Now would be the perfect time to tell him, she decided, until he wrapped her in a huge towel, picked her up and returned to the bedroom to lay her across the tangled sheets. When Georgie opened her mouth to speak, he kissed her again. Passion precluded any admissions and, after Austin had the condom in place, the lovemaking began again.

This time Austin moved atop her, guided himself inside her and moved in a tempered rhythm. Georgie ran her hands over his damp back, held on close and listened to the sound of his labored breaths.

Oh, how she cherished the moments right before

he climaxed. Oh, how much she cherished him. And when he tensed with his release, the words clamored out of her mouth. "I love you, Austin."

He stilled against her for a moment, then rolled onto his back. She waited for a response, and the one she received was extremely unexpected.

"It was always you, Georgie."

She shifted to her side. "Meaning?"

"The demise of my marriage. Abby never measured up to you. No woman ever has. I've known that for a long time, but I didn't want to admit that you have that much control over me. Call it stupid pride or male ego or however you want to label it. I'm over it now."

Georgie couldn't recall a time when she'd felt so optimistic, yet so fearful when she considered the impending declaration. "You've always been the only man for me. Actually, you've been the only man I've made love with."

He lifted his head and frowned. "Seriously?"

"Seriously."

He slid his arm beneath her and brought her against his chest. "I'm honored, Georgie. And dammit, I love you, too."

She laid a palm over his beating heart, the first hint of tears welling in her eyes. "Seriously?"

"More than my best roping horse. More than my money or all my material wealth. More than I realized until now."

Georgie began to silently rehearse how she would tell him about Chance and her explanation as to why she had withheld the truth for so long. Feeling as ready as she would ever be, she lifted to her head and whispered, "Austin."

He didn't open his eyes, didn't stir a bit. From the rise and fall of his chest, she determined he'd fallen asleep.

Georgie laid her cheek back on his chest, her emotions a blend of relief and regret that she hadn't spoken when she'd had the chance. But she would still have the opportunity once he finally awoke. In the meantime, she would join him in a nap and hope that when the revelations finally came, he would find it in his heart to forgive her, and embrace fathering their son.

An annoying sound jarred Austin out of sleep for the second time in twenty-four hours, only this time it was a buzzer, not a horn. He worked his arm from beneath Georgie, kissed her cheek then went into the bathroom to clean up. He grabbed a T-shirt and jeans from the closet, got dressed quickly and entered the bedroom where Georgie was sitting up against the leather headboard, clutching the sheet to her chin.

"Where are you going?" she asked as he headed toward the door.

The bell rang again, letting him know that the unknown intruder hadn't left. "I'm going to see who's at the door and send them on their way."

"Okay. Hurry back."

Exactly what he planned to do. He strode through the great room and once he reached the entry, he peered out the peephole. Jenny stood on the porch with a paper sack in hand, looking determined as ever. He doubted she would leave anytime soon, which drove him to yank open the door and scowl. "What's up?"

She patted her big blond hair and smiled. "Well, sugar, since you and Georgie didn't come for lunch, lunch is coming to you."

He felt the need to preserve Georgie's reputation. "What makes you think I'm not alone?"

She nodded toward the driveway. "Because that's her truck, sweetie. And don't worry. I'll just hand this over and be on my way."

Austin took the bag and worked up some gratitude. "Thanks. I appreciate the hospitality."

Jenny centered her gaze on his bare feet before focusing on his face. "And I'm sure Georgie appreciates your hospitality, as well. You two enjoy the rest of your afternoon. If you're in the mood for a drink, you know where to find me."

After Jen spun on her heels and stepped off the porch, Austin waited until she'd climbed onto the golf cart and drove away toward the main house. He shut and locked the door, then walked toward the kitchen to drop off the care package before returning to the bedroom. He discovered Georgie seated at the island, dressed in the only robe he owned—a heavy blue flannel that hung off her like a scarecrow.

He set the sack down at the end of the quartz counter and claimed the stool beside her. "Guess you figured out the identity of our guests."

She tightened the sash at her waist. "I kind of heard Jen's voice."

No shock there. "She brought food. Are you hungry?"

She ran a fingertip along the edge of the island. "Not at the moment, but feel free to go ahead."

He sensed something was bugging her. Maybe he'd said too much in the moment. "Are you okay, Georgie?"

When she lifted her gaze to his, he saw a few tears welling in her eyes. "Actually, I'm not okay. I have something I need to tell you. Something I should have told you long before now."

A laundry list of possibilities bombarded his brain. One horrible conclusion came home to roost. "Are you sick?"

She shook her head. "No, that's not it. Not even close."

"Then what is it?"

"Just promise me you won't be too angry."

"I'll try, but that depends on what you're about to tell me."

She fidgeted in the seat, a sure sign of her nervousness. After a deep breath, she said, "Okay. Here goes. I have a five-year-old son."

Austin didn't know what to say or how to react. He did recall with absolute clarity what she'd said to him earlier.

...you've been the only man I've made love with...

The mental impact hit Austin like a grenade, sending him off the stool to pace. Shock gave way to confusion then melted into blinding anger. He turned around to confront her head-on, grasping the last shred of his composure. He had a burning question to ask, although he suspected he already knew the answer. "Who's his father, Georgie?"

Her tears flowed freely now, and she looked away before returning her attention to him. "You are, Austin."

Georgie held her breath and waited, wanting so badly to plead with him to give her a chance to explain. Instead, she remained silent and watchful as he braced his elbows on the table, lowered his eyes and forked both hands through his hair.

"Why the hell didn't you tell me sooner?" he asked without looking up.

"I tried, Austin."

"Obviously not too damn hard, Georgie."

She deserved his scorn, but she wouldn't stop attempting to make him understand. "When I found out I was pregnant, I was pretty much in denial for a couple of months until I finally confirmed it. Then I called your cell phone and some woman answered. I thought I had the wrong number, so I got in touch with Dallas. He told me you'd just married. I was so in shock over the baby, and learning you'd found someone else, I didn't know what to do."

He straightened and leveled a stern stare on her. "You should've called back. You should've told me immediately."

"I considered that, but when I decided not to give Chance up for adoption, I realized that if I told you, I might ruin your relationship."

"And you thought it was okay just to leave me in the dark?"

"Believe me, I've questioned my actions since the day he was born."

"You damn sure should have," he said, barely concealed venom in his tone. "And no matter what excuse you try to hand me, you had no right to keep this a secret."

"I know." She paused a moment to gather her thoughts. "He's an incredible little boy, and so much like you. He loves the horses and he's so smart. If you'll get to know him, I'm sure—"

"You need to leave, Georgie."

So much for that strategy. "I'm not leaving until we discuss this further."

"I don't want to discuss anything right now. I'm

too damned angry. Just put on your clothes and go home."

She would grant him this latitude for the time being. "Fine," she said as she came to her feet. "I'll go for now, and I'll wait to hear from you. And if I don't, have a nice life. Chance and I have done fine without you. We'll continue to do the same."

Georgie rushed past him and into the bedroom, holding fast to her sadness until she returned to the safety of her home. After she dressed, she returned to the kitchen, but Austin was nowhere to be found. She didn't bother to seek him out, or attempt to convince him that his little boy needed him. He would have to come to that conclusion on his own.

She would give Austin more time, pray he came around and learn to accept that he might not. She only hoped that she could grant her son's wish, and he'd finally have a daddy for Christmas. If not, she would continue to love him enough for the both of them.

Nine

"I'm so sorry I'm late."

Georgie looked up from the menu at Paris, who was struggling to be seated in the booth of the small San Antonio bistro. "That's okay. How did the appointment go?"

Paris set her bag aside and tightened the band securing her low ponytail. "That's why I'm late. The doctor decided to do a last-minute ultrasound."

"Is everything all right?"

"Yes, aside from the fact that if I reach my due date, the baby will weigh at least eight pounds. No wonder I'm so huge."

"You look great, especially in that dress. Green is definitely your color."

"I look like a giant jalapeno pepper." Paris leaned over and studied her. "You look like you're exhausted."

She was, mentally and physically. "I haven't been sleeping."

"But you have been crying. A lot."

Clearly her reddened eyes had given her away. "I didn't know it was that obvious."

Paris leaned over and touched her arm. "Tell me what's wrong."

Georgie didn't want to burden a very pregnant woman, but she could certainly use a friend. "It's Austin."

"You told him."

"I did, and it didn't go well." She hadn't heard a word from him since.

Leaning back, Paris rested her arm across her rounded belly. "That explains it."

"Explains what?"

"Austin took off yesterday morning for heaven knows where and he didn't come back last night. When Dallas sent him a text, he replied that he was okay, and that's it. And you haven't heard from him, either?"

"I sent him a text to ask if he was okay," Georgie said. "He responded 'no,' and I decided to leave him alone."

Paris seemed surprised. "You didn't try calling him?"

She'd thought about it, several times. "In all the years I've known Austin, I've learned you don't back him into a corner. Usually after he thinks things over, he comes around."

"That's good," Paris stated. "I'm sure he'll be back in touch soon."

If only Georgie could believe that. "He might not this time. He's angry and he's hurt and I have to accept that he could reject the prospect of being a father to Chance."

"Austin is a good man, Georgie. I can't imagine him abandoning his own flesh and blood."

"I hope that's true, but you didn't see the look on his face when I told him. He was furious, understandably so."

"You honestly don't believe he'll get over it?"

She thought back through the years and couldn't recall a time when he'd been so irate. "When we were kids, and he got mad at me for some reason, he wouldn't leave until we worked it out. He'd make self-deprecating comments about his ignorance and a few bad jokes, and before I knew it, I was laughing and all was forgiven."

"The Calloway brothers must share the brooding gene," Paris said. "That's exactly what Dallas did when he learned, as did I, that I wasn't officially divorced and he stood to lose control of the ranch to Fort because our marriage wasn't real. Fortunately, Jenny saved the day on that count."

Her interest piqued, Georgie rested her elbow on the table and supported her cheek on her palm. "So how did you manage to convince Dallas to come back to you?"

Paris laughed. "It wasn't me. The family gave him a swift kick in the jeans and booted him to right here, in San Antonio, to beg my forgiveness. The rest, as they say, is history. Now I'm happily married to the love of my life, for the second time, and about to give birth to a baby apparently the size of a moose."

Georgie smiled for the first time in two days. "Hopefully the doctor is wrong about the baby's weight."

"And hopefully you're wrong about Austin. I wouldn't be surprised if he reaches out to you soon."

Georgie sat back and sighed. "I would love it if that happens before Sunday."

"Then you could all be a family on Christmas," Paris said in a wistful tone.

"And I could answer a little boy's wish. Chance asked Santa if he would bring him a daddy."

Paris's expression turned somber. "Oh, Georgie. That must have broken your heart. How much does he know about Austin?"

Georgie shrugged. "Very little. He didn't ask a whole lot until about a year ago, and I attribute that to being in preschool and noticing everyone else has a father. I've only mentioned that his dad lives far away, which I thought he did at the time, and that he travels a lot because he's a cowboy."

"Does he know his name?"

"He asked right before he left for Florida, and then he became distracted by something on TV. I'm sure he'll ask again when he gets home." Georgie had given Lila specific instructions to direct Chance to her with any queries, and she had no reason to believe her mother wouldn't comply.

"And you'll know what to do if and when that happens." Paris began to scan the menu. "I'm starving. What are you having?"

A strong urge to call her mom and check on her baby boy. "Probably just a Cobb salad. I'm not very hungry."

Paris closed the menu and set it aside. "I'm going to have the spinach enchilada plate and eat every last bite. And after that, I might even eat dessert. Gotta feed the moose."

They joined in a laugh before the waiter arrived to take their orders. Once he left, Georgie regarded Paris. "As soon as we're finished with lunch, I'm going to go shopping. I haven't bought a thing for Chance, aside from a pony, and I can't put her under the tree."

Paris sipped at her glass of water. "Where did you get a pony?"

"The Carter ranch right outside Cotulla. She's fifteen years old and her name is Butterball, which fits her well. She'll be a good teaching horse for Chance, although I'm sure he'll want to graduate to something bigger very soon."

"That's great, and I could pick up a few more holiday gifts. I could also use a stroll on the River Walk to burn a few calories."

"Great. We'll make an afternoon of it."

Paris sent her a soft smile. "And with your permission, I'll see what I can do about Austin on my end."

Georgie saw more than a few problems with that scenario. "He'll be furious if he knows I told you about Chance before I told him."

"That's too bad. Besides, I'll let him assume you told me today. If he's going to pout like a child, then I'll just sic Dallas on him. Better still, I'll involve Maria, as long as you're okay with it."

She wasn't sure she was, but then again, what other options did she have? If the Calloways could convince Austin to step up to the plate, then maybe that would be best for the sake of her son. No amount of cajoling on their part would change Austin's mind about what she'd done. "I assume you're referring to a family meeting."

"Exactly. Power in numbers."

Georgie imagined Austin encountering his stepmothers and brothers in a showdown. She would definitely buy tickets to that.

Austin walked through his front door to find Paris, Dallas, Jenny and Maria seated on his leather sectional in the great room. He should never have told them he was heading home. He should never have given out spare keys.

After tossing his duffel onto the floor, he gave them all a good glare. "Mind telling me what you're doing here?"

Maria patted the space between her and Jenny. "Come have a seat, *mijo*."

No way would he suffer maternal advice in stereo. "I'll stand, thank you."

Dallas rose from the sofa where he'd been positioned next to his wife. "Makes no difference to any of us whether you sit or stand. We're more concerned with your total lack of responsibility to your family."

His foul mood grew even fouler. "I didn't know building a house on our land came with a clause that states I can't come and go as I please."

"We were worried about you, sugar," Jenny said. "You've been gone four days with almost no communication. That's not like you."

And to think he'd worried someone had found out about his and Georgie's kid. "I wasn't intentionally ignoring you all. I just have another business to run. Several, in fact."

"We're referring to your responsibility to your son."

Damn if he hadn't had cause to worry and wonder exactly how this all went down. "Did Georgie also tell you that she hid him from me for five years?"

"Georgie didn't talk to them," Paris piped up. "She talked to me, and I told Dallas. Dallas told everyone else."

His shortened fuse was about to blow. "When it comes right down to it, this isn't anyone's business."

Maria looked fit to be tied. "It is our business, Austin Calloway. Maybe I'm not your birth mother, son, but I'm the only mother you've had for thirty-two years. That means I consider that little boy my grandchild."

"Mine, too," Jenny said. "At least that's how I see him, even if we're not blood relatives, either. But I'd like to borrow him until Worth and Fort have children."

Maria sent her an acid glare. "As long as you give him back."

Jenny ignored the dig. "Regardless, that little boy deserves to know our family, sugar."

Austin had agonized over that since Georgie spilled the baby beans. He'd been torn between a permanent escape and meeting the child who didn't know him at all. "Look, I've got a lot to think about before we plan a family reunion."

"Georgie's a wreck, Austin," Paris added. "She's beginning to believe you don't want to have anything to do with Chance."

Just one more blow to his and Georgie's relationship. "I'll be sure to thank her for nominating me for jerk of the year."

Maria suddenly rose from the sofa. "Everyone, go about your business. I want to talk to Austin alone."

What Maria wanted, Maria got, and that was apparent by the way everyone stood and started milling toward the door. Everyone but Jenny.

His stepmom stared at the other stepmother for a moment. "That means everyone."

Jenny lifted her chin. "I'm not going anywhere until Austin asks me to leave."

He didn't care if the Pope made an appearance. "Fine by me if you stay. In fact, you can all hang around and crucify me."

Dallas pressed a palm against his wife's back. "We're going home to spend some alone time together. The phones will be turned off."

Paris blushed. "A little too much information, Dallas."

"Who cares?" Dallas said. "It's pretty obvious by looking at you, we've done it before."

Dallas and Paris rushed out the door, leaving Austin alone to face the mothers—Maria wearing her trademark braid and a long green flannel shirt over her jeans, and Jen sporting a red-checkered dress and a matching bow in her big blond hair. Nothing like a verbal beating from a hardscrabble rancher's wife and a throwback from a fifties sitcom. He'd rather eat Nueces River mud.

Austin claimed the cowhide chair across from the

sofa, determined to make this little soiree short and sweet. "Speak your mind, then give me some peace."

Jenny sent him a sympathetic look. "I know you're torn up about this, sugar."

"I also know you're mad as hell at Georgie, too," Maria began, "and I don't think anyone blames you for that. But she's always been a good girl and from what I hear, a good mother. If I were you, I'd march to her house right now, meet your son and make amends with Georgie."

If only it was that easy. "Neither of you know what I've been going through since she told me. I kept thinking about the things I've missed, like his first steps and his first words. I could've already taught him how to ride. How to throw a rope. Georgie robbed me of those experiences."

"It's not too late to make memories now, Austin," Jenny said. "I don't care how good of a job Georgie's done raising him as a single mother, that little boy needs his daddy. And you need him and his mother, too."

Austin leaned forward and streaked both palms over his face. "I know you're both right, and I plan to be involved in his life, pay child support, that kind of thing. But I don't know if I can ever forgive Georgie."

Maria frowned. "Why not? She's forgiven you."

They seemed determined to make this all his fault. "What did I do?"

"It's not what you did, sugar," Jenny added. "It's what you didn't do."

He recalled Georgie saying the same thing. "I'm not following you, Jen."

"After playing slap and tickle with her all during high school, did you stay in touch with Georgie, sugar?"

"No, but—"

"After you made a baby while passing through town, did you ever call her?" Maria asked.

He recognized where this was going. "Georgie knew we weren't exclusive, and besides, I met Abby right after that."

"And married a woman you barely knew, totally ignoring the other woman who's loved you since you pulled her ponytail the first time," Maria said. "We all know how that turned out."

He'd always appreciated Maria's brutal honesty, until tonight. Being on the hot seat with all his faults laid bare wasn't his idea of a good time.

Jenny smoothed a palm over her skirt. "I truly believe we only have one love in our lives, and your father was mine and, I assume, Maria's. However, J.D.'s one true love happened to be your mother."

"She's right," Maria added, much to Austin's surprise. "Your dad kept searching to fill that hole in his soul from losing Carol. I'd bet my best spurs that Georgie is your soul mate, and you're going to spend a lot of useless years if you don't own up to it."

Austin wanted to reject their notions. "I can't believe the two of you can overlook the fact that he was married to both of you at the same time. Hell, he spread himself so thin he wasn't giving anyone the time they needed, including his six sons."

"You're absolutely right, sugar," Jenny said. "All the more reason for you to resolve the issues with Georgie and get busy spending time with your little boy."

His head had begun to spin from all the unwelcome advice. "I'll consider what you've said, but right now I have to take care of the horses. So if you two don't mind, I need to get on with my day."

"Okay." Maria came to her feet. "*Mijo*, you need to learn that if you really love someone, nothing they do or say is beyond forgiveness."

Jen rose from the sofa. "Sugar, the best holiday gift you can give yourself is a happy New Year with a new family."

Without another word, the mothers walked out the door, blanketing the room in stark silence. Austin leaned back in the chair and felt compelled to revisit his past. He stood and walked to the shelves flanking the white stone fireplace, then withdrew his final high school yearbook. He returned to the sofa and once again flipped through the pages, finding various photos of Georgie scattered throughout. He appreciated the one of her holding the volleyball district MVP trophy when everyone had told her she was too short to play. The one when she'd been voted to represent the junior class in the homecoming court was really something else, but then so was she dressed in that blue shiny dress, her long hair curling over her shoulders. He also hated that Rory Mills had been on her arm during the halftime festivities, while he'd escorted the senior queen, Heather Daws, who was about as shallow as a dried-up lake.

It suddenly dawned on him that not once had they appeared in a picture together, all because of an ongoing family feud and his resistance to rocking the boat. If he'd only stood up to his father, and hers, things might have been different between them. Or not. Maybe they'd been destined to go their separate ways, choose their own paths, make their own lives. Maybe his failed marriage had taught him what he didn't want—a relationship that would never live up to what he'd had with Georgie. But did he really deserve her now?

When a knock came at the door, Austin set the book on the coffee table and shot to his feet, anxious to see if maybe Georgie had stopped by. He was sorely disappointed to find a sibling standing on the threshold.

"Did I miss it?" Worth asked.

"Miss what?"

"The family meeting."

Dallas obviously told every last Calloway about his plight. "Yep. It's over."

"Mind if I come in for a bit?"

"Why not?" He didn't have anything better to do except sit around, feeling sorry for himself.

Worth brushed past him, dropped down on the sofa and eyed the yearbook. "Looks like you've been reliving your glory days."

He hadn't found any glory in the experience. "Just feeling nostalgic."

"Mom tells me you were a jock. Something about all-district wide receiver."

Austin had never been comfortable talking about his accolades. "It wasn't a big deal. My high school was so small there wasn't a whole lot of competition."

Worth forked a hand through his blond hair. "I know what you mean. I went to a private school. We didn't even have a football team, but I did play basketball. Our team pretty much sucked most of the time."

Austin was growing increasingly irritated by the small talk. "It happens. Look, I hate to cut this conversation short, but I have some chores to tend to."

"No problem. But before I go, I just have one thing to say about your current situation."

Just what he needed, more sage advice from a self-proclaimed Louisiana rodeo cowboy surfer. "Shoot."

"I know you've had everyone coming at you with suggestions on how to handle this news, but I just want you to know that if you want to talk, feel free to find me. No advice. No judgment."

That nearly shocked Austin out of his boots. "I appreciate that."

"What are brothers for? Besides, you'll figure it out."

"I'm not so sure about that."

"You're a smart guy, Austin. In fact, intelligence is a Calloway trait, although some of us intentionally don't show it."

"You've got to be pretty smart to build a fleet of charter boats all down the coast, Worth."

"I've been lucky in business. I just thank my lucky stars I didn't head down my original career path."

"Rodeo?"

"Medical school."

Now he was downright stunned. "I didn't know that."

"Most people don't. I swore my mom to secrecy after she bragged I was accepted to every Ivy League school I applied to. She was damn disappointed when I decided to stay in Louisiana and went to Tulane. She was proud of my 4.0 GPA as a chemistry major."

Austin wasn't sure he could take any more revelations. "No offense, Worth, but I've never pegged you as a science geek."

Worth stood and grinned. "I figured out early on it's best to dumb it down a bit when it comes to courting women. Take care, bud."

Austin came to his feet. "You, too, Worth. Are you going to be around during the holidays?"

"Nope. I'm going to Maui. I'd invite you along but I figure you've got more pressing issues at the moment."

"You're right about that," Austin said as he followed his brother to the door.

Worth paused with his hand on the knob. "You know, Austin, we're not our dad. Not by a long shot. Except maybe Fort. As bad as he hated J.D., he's the most like him. Mom hopes he'll eventually come around, but I've given up on that ever happening."

So had the rest of the family. "Happy holidays and have a good trip."

"Same to you, and when I get back, I look forward to meeting my nephew."

He might have been mad at Worth for tossing in that veiled recommendation, but in all honesty, his half brother had been the most helpful.

Austin settled back on the sofa and rolled all his options around in his head. Truth was, he did love Georgie and probably always had. He wanted to know his son and to avoid all the mistakes his own father had made. He still wanted to marry the love of his life…but what if he failed?

That in itself was his greatest fear, but maybe the time had come to stop being a relationship coward. First he had to decide if, when and where he would present the plan to Georgie, and hope that he hadn't waited too long.

When Georgie pulled into the drive, she was thrilled to see her mother and Chance waiting for her on the front porch. She'd barely exited the truck before Chance ran to her and threw his arms around her waist.

He smiled up at her. "Hi, Mama."

She leaned down and hugged him hard. "Hi, sweetie. I missed you so much! I think you grew two inches while you were gone."

His eyes went wide as he stepped out of her grasp. "Did I?"

"I believe you did." She looked around but didn't see the motor home. "Where're Uncle Ben and Aunt Debbie?"

Her mother approached and ruffled Chance's hair. "They took off for Arizona to see the grandkids. They told me to tell you bye and what a pleasure it was to have your son along for the trip."

"I'm sorry I wasn't here to thank them," Georgie said as Chance ran back into the house. "I didn't expect you for another hour or so, and I had an emergency at the Rileys' farm. I had to treat a colicky mare."

"That's okay. You can give them a call later."

"Do you need a ride home?"

"No. Your father should be here any minute now."

Georgie was quite surprised by the news. "You mean he's actually going to step foot on his daughter's property?"

"Yes, and he wants to talk to you."

After everything that had happened with Austin,

Georgie didn't have the energy for a fight. "I'm not up to that right now."

"Well, I suppose you should get up for that because this conversation is long overdue."

Before Georgie could respond, the familiar ancient white truck headed up the gravel drive, signaling her patriarch had arrived. She experienced a case of butterflies in the pit of her stomach and her palms began to sweat, despite the fact that the cold front had arrived in earnest, bringing with it forty-degree temps.

She had no clue what she would say to the man who'd raised her, and ignored her for five years. A hard-nosed man who could be as stubborn as a mule. A man who had never even seen his own grandchild. At least she had an ally in his wife.

Her mother began to back away as soon as the truck came to a stop in front of the house. "I'll keep Chance occupied while you two chat."

"But Mom—"

"You'll be okay, honey. Just hear him out."

Lila turned around and started away, while Georgie held her breath and waited for George Romero to appear. And he did a few moments later, looking every bit the brown-eyed hulking cowboy, only his hair seemed a little grayer and his gait a little slower. He'd always been larger than life, her hero, and she'd always been his little girl, until she'd shamed him by having a child out of wedlock. Heaven only knew what he would've done had he known the identity of Chance's father.

"Dad," she said when he walked up to her.

"Georgie," he replied, tattered beige hat in hand.

So far, so good. "You look well. How's your back?"

"Stiff as usual, but it's nothing compared to the scare I had with the old ticker last month."

That was news to her, and very disconcerting. "Mom didn't say a word to me about you having heart problems."

"I told her not to say anything until I could tell you myself."

"Is it serious?"

"Just some minor blockage. They did one of those angioplasty procedures and stuck some sort of tube in my artery. Now I'm good as new."

"I'm so sorry." And she was. "I wish I would've known."

"The only thing you need to know is I had a wake-up call. I've been a fool and prideful and a sorry excuse for a father. That comes to an end today."

"I appreciate that, Daddy."

That earned her a grin. "Been a long time since you called me that. I love you, princess. And I'm done being an old stubborn goat. I'm ready to meet my grandboy."

That earned him a hug. "I'm so glad we have this behind us. Chance needs his grandfather a lot. He hasn't had a solid male influence for five years."

Her father's expression melted into a frown. "No surprise there. Austin Calloway is a no-account tail chaser, just like his dad."

Clearly Lila hadn't hidden Georgie's secrets. "How long have you known?"

"When your mother told me you were coming back to town. She has some crazy idea that you and Calloway are going to set up house and raise your son together."

Considering she hadn't heard a word from Austin, that was highly unlikely. "Did Mom also tell you that Austin was unaware that he had a child?"

He inclined his head and studied her straight on. "Was?"

"I told him about Chance a few days ago."

"Is the jackass here?"

She shook her head. "No, he's not here. He's still trying to get over the shock."

He sent her a skeptic's look. "If you believe that, then I've got some swampland to sell you."

After what her father had done to her, Georgie felt the need to defend Austin. "You're wrong about him, Dad. He's a good man."

"He wasn't man enough to ask permission to date you when you two were in school. He just continued to sneak around behind my back."

Lila had evidently provided a wealth of knowledge. "Neither of us wanted to tell you or J.D. because you two were still acting like kindergarten rivals."

"That's because J.D. tried to…" Both his words and gaze faltered. "Never mind."

"Not fair, Dad. You apparently know about my life, now it's time you tell me more about yours. What did J.D. do to you aside from compete in the cattle business?"

"He dated your mother before me," he muttered.

Georgie couldn't hold back a laugh. "That's it? You two had an ongoing feud because J.D. went out with Mom? That's rich considering you married her. And best I can recall, he married Carol."

He shook out his hat and shoved it on his head. "I'm ready to get off this subject and get on with the business of meeting my grandson."

"I'm all for that."

Georgie led him to the house where he followed her through the front door. They came upon Chance hanging ornaments on the Christmas tree she'd purchased yesterday, a seven-foot fragrant pine that had been the last decent selection on the lot.

"Hey, little man," she said. "I have someone I want you to meet."

Chance hooked a red globe over one limb, turned around and stared in awe. "Are you my dad?"

Lila smiled. "No, sweetheart, but he's the next best thing. This is your grandpa."

"Grandpa George?" he asked without a hint of

disappointment in his tone. "My grandma said you were gone a lot."

Her dad stepped forward and took off his hat. "Yep, I've been gone far too long. And you must be Chance."

Her son nodded his head and grinned. "Chance William Romero."

"Well, bud, looks like you've got my middle name," George said in an awed tone. "Do you like to go fishin'?"

"Haven't gone fishin' yet," Chance said.

Amazingly, the grandfather took his grandson's hand and led him to the sofa. "Let's sit a spell and I'll tell you all about how to cast a line…"

Georgie began to finish the decorating tasks, all the while counting her blessings over the scene playing out before her. She'd almost given up believing that her dad would accept his grandson, much less begin a precious relationship with him. And if any more time passed, she would be forced to give up on Austin.

She wondered if it might be too much to ask for one more holiday miracle.

Ten

It would take a miracle if Austin survived this visit without incurring Georgie's wrath. For the past five days, he'd developed a plan that could smooth over his disregard, if she didn't kick him off her rented ranch.

Before he could climb out of the truck, his cell sounded, and he didn't even have to look to see who might be calling. If he ignored it, he'd have hell to pay. If he answered, he would only be further delayed. He answered it anyway.

"Yeah, Jen?"

"Have you done it yet?"

"I just got here."

"Oh, good. If all goes well, Maria and I want you to invite everyone to dinner."

He might not even get in the front door. "You're jumping the gun a little there. I don't even know if Georgie will see me yet."

"She will, sugar. Best of luck and we'll see you, Georgie and the little guy soon."

Before he could debate that point, Jen, with her overblown optimism, hung up. Now he had to return to the starting line and begin the mental race to the finish.

Gathering all his courage, he exited the truck and sprinted up the steps to the porch. He checked his back pocket for the gift, rehearsed what he planned to say and then finally knocked.

He expected Georgie to open the door, but what he got was her mother. Not a good way to begin his groveling.

Lila laid a hand beneath her throat like she might start choking. "Oh, my. Hello, Austin."

He took off his hat and nodded. "Nice to see you ma'am. Is Georgie here?"

"Yes. It's Christmas morning."

Good going, Calloway. "Mind if I have a word with her?"

"Wait here and I'll go get her."

He wasn't exactly surprised that he hadn't been invited in, and that was probably best. If George Romero happened to be there, Austin would risk getting a right hook as a greeting.

He paced around the porch for a few minutes until he heard, "What are you doing here, Austin?"

When he turned around, Austin would swear his heart skipped several beats, and it had nothing to do with his giant case of the nerves. Just seeing Georgie again served to confirm he had done the right thing, even if the end result could include her rejection.

He decided to lay it all on the line, beginning with their child. "I did a lot of soul-searching over the past few days, and I've come to the conclusion that I've already missed too much time with our son."

She folded her arms across her middle. "I'm glad. He needs to get to know you before he's any older."

One issue resolved, several more to go. "I plan to start on that immediately, and you need to be aware that I'm going to be there to support him and not only financially. I want to be part of his life in every way, including school and whatever extracurricular activities he chooses to do, and I'm banking on teaching him to rope."

He saw a mix of happiness and disappointment in her eyes. "That all sounds wonderful, Austin. We can work together to give him a good life. You can count on me to be cooperative when it comes to visitation. We'll work out a schedule."

She didn't understand he didn't give a damn about a schedule, but she would. "I haven't covered the most important aspect of our arrangement."

"Then please, continue," she said in a frigid tone.

"First, I have a question. Is your dad in the house?"

She looked confused. "Yes, but—"

"Could you send him out here?"

"Are you sure you want to do that?"

Not really. "Yeah. I have to talk to him before we continue this conversation."

"All right, I'll try. But I can't guarantee he'll do it."

If Old George wanted to be pigheaded, he'd have to go in after him. Fortunately that didn't happen when Georgie went inside and returned with her dad in tow, looking none too pleased to be there.

"Merry Christmas, sir," Austin said, even though he realized the man didn't look like he embraced the holiday spirit.

"What do you want, Calloway?" George asked, confirming Austin's theory.

"I have a question to ask you before I finish my talk with Georgie."

"Let me make this easy on you. No, I don't want you here, and yes, you should get in that fancy truck and head for the hills."

"Behave, Dad," Georgie scolded. "You can at least hear what he has to say before you send him packing."

"Fine," George said grudgingly. "But make it quick."

He drew in a breath and released it slowly. "Mr. Romero, I've screwed up a time or two in my life, but my biggest mistake was letting Georgie go without a fight, even if it meant going into battle against you and my dad. Hell, when she didn't meet me that day I left for college, I should have come looking for her."

Georgie touched his arm. "What are you talking about?"

"I went to your house and gave your mom a card that asked you to meet me at the old windmill. I planned to invite you to join me at school once you graduated."

"I never got that card," she said, anger in her tone. "I definitely have a bone to pick with Mom."

"I tore it up," George muttered, drawing both their attention.

Now Georgie looked furious. "Excuse me, Dad?"

"You heard me. I took it from your mother, read it and shredded it." He pointed at Austin. "You should be glad I didn't know you were taking her behind the shed."

That explained a lot, and fed Austin's resentment toward this man. But in the interest of keeping the peace, he tempered his anger. "As pissed off as I am over your actions, it really doesn't matter now. What's done is done. We can't go back." Although he wished they could.

"Yes, it does matter," Georgie said. "I've always blamed you for not saying goodbye before you took off for college. Why didn't you tell me this before now?"

Austin shrugged. "I thought you had your reasons, the main one being we were on different paths. I figured you decided our relationship had run its course."

"If I had known, I would have been there."

Austin wanted to kiss her, but he still had business to tend to. "Back to the question at hand." He turned to Georgie's dad. "Mr. Romero, I'm going to ask for your daughter's hand in marriage, and if she decides to accept my proposal, I hope we have your and Mrs. Romero's blessing."

Georgie stared and George glared, while Austin just stood there, waiting for someone to speak. Her dad came through first. "I'd like to tell you hell no, you're not going to get my blessing, but you're going to do what you want anyway, so go for it. As far as my wife is concerned, she had visions of the two of you hitched the minute Georgie came back to town. Now get your proposing out of the way before your boy wakes up and wonders if his mama ran off with Santa."

When the man returned inside, Austin decided to proceed as planned, even though he worried Georgie's continuing silence indicated she wasn't too keen on the idea. He'd find out real soon.

He pulled the box from his pocket and set it on the railing, then withdrew the ring before turning to Georgie. "Darlin', there is no one else on this earth that I want to wake up to every morning and go to bed with every night. I've made my share of mistakes, but having you as my wife wouldn't be one of them. I'd be proud and honored if you would marry me."

"This marriage proposal isn't because of Chance, is it?" she asked, the first sign of tears in her eyes.

"No, sweetheart. I want to spend my life with you because I love you. Always have. Always will."

"And you're absolutely sure you want to do this marriage thing again?"

"Sure as sunrise."

"I can be a handful."

"So can I. But together, we're pretty damn perfect."

Finally, she smiled. "Then yes, Austin Calloway, I will marry you, with or without my father's blessing. I love you, too. Very much."

"That's all I need to hear." Smiling, he slid the sapphire-and-diamond ring on her finger and waited for her response to the surprise.

She studied it for a moment before recognition dawned in her expression and her gaze shot to his. "This is the ring from the silent auction. I had no idea you bid on it."

"I didn't. I had to hunt down the guy who won it and pay twice the amount to take it off his hands when I saw how much you wanted it that night. I may not have consciously believed it would be an engagement ring, but deep down I probably realized that it should be."

She threw her arms around his neck, then kissed him soundly. "You're too much. And this is too much."

The joy in her eyes said it all. "Darlin', nothing is too much for my future bride. But before we make this official, I probably need to ask the little man's permission, too."

She placed a hand to her mouth. "I hadn't thought about Chance. I think we should probably ease him into the idea. Meeting you on Christmas morning is a lot for a five-year-old to handle."

His first lesson in fatherhood. "Let's just play it by ear."

She let him go and reached for the door. "Are you ready?"

"As ready as I'll ever be."

Austin followed Georgie inside and surveyed the room, only to discover George seated in a chair, watching some cartoon on the TV mounted over a fireplace decked out with stockings. The Christmas tree positioned in the corner had been decorated in red and green, and a slew of unopened presents reminded Austin of what he'd forgotten.

"I'll be right back," he said as he headed outside and sprinted to the truck, then returned with the first gift for his son. He planned to give him many more—the most important, his time.

When he heard voices, a woman's and a child's, he clutched the package and waited anxiously for the moment he laid his eyes on his son. He didn't have to wait long before a brown-haired, hazel-eyed boy wearing pajamas dotted with bucking broncos padded into the room. Austin's first reaction—he looked just like his mother. His second—he couldn't have imagined the impact on his emotions. He hadn't known he would feel so strongly. He couldn't be more proud to be his dad. He only hoped his son shared his feelings.

With Lila following behind him, Chance pulled up short the second he spotted Austin, then he grinned. "You're that guy we saw at the calf roping. Mama's friend."

Before Austin could respond, Georgie gestured Chance to her, turned him around and rested her hands on his shoulders. "This is Austin Calloway, Chance. Austin, meet Chance."

He hesitated a moment before he approached slowly and knelt at his child's level. "It's great to finally meet you, bud. This is for you."

Chance took the offered present and looked it over. "Can I open it now?"

Austin turned his attention to Georgie who nodded. "Go ahead."

The boy tore into the package in record time, then pulled out the baseball glove from the box. "Wow. I don't have one of these."

"My dad gave me that when I was about your

age," Austin said. "I figure we can play a little catch someday soon."

Chance wrinkled his nose. "Won't your dad be mad 'cause you gave it to me?"

He didn't have the heart to tell his son that he wouldn't ever know his grandfather. "Nope," he said as he straightened. "He'd be pleased."

Georgie ruffled Chance's hair. "Sweetie, before we open the rest of your gifts, we need to have a little talk."

Chance glanced back at her. "Aw, Mom. Do we hafta?"

She smiled. "Yes, but this has to do with something you wanted from Santa."

"A pony?" he asked.

"We'll get to that later," Georgie said. "Mom, Dad, do you mind if we have a few minutes alone?"

"Come on, George," Lila said. "You can help me make breakfast for a change."

George stood and muttered under his breath as he followed his wife out of the living room.

Georgie swept her hand toward the navy-colored sofa. "Let's have a seat."

After they settled in with Chance between them, Austin regarded Georgie. "Do you want me to go first?"

"I think you should," she said, wariness in her tone.

Austin shifted slightly so he could gauge his son's

reaction. "Chance, I've known your mom for a long time. We went to school together."

"Kindergarten?" he asked.

"Yep, and all the way through high school."

"We were boyfriend and girlfriend," Georgie added. "Do you know what that is?"

Chance sent them both a sour look. "Yeah. That means you kissed and stuff."

After she and Austin exchanged a smile, Georgie continued. "Austin and I cared about each other very much. We still do."

When Georgie went silent and looked at him, Austin figured that was his cue. "I'm not only your mama's friend, bud, I'm your dad."

Chance stared at him without speaking, then his smile came out of hiding. "Santa sent you to me?"

Austin chuckled. "I guess you could say that, seeing how it's Christmas morning. How do you feel about this?"

"Are you a real live cowboy?"

"I guess you could say that, too."

"He's a calf roping champion, Chance," Georgie chimed in. "He has lots of trophies."

"Can I see them?"

"Sure," Austin said. "I plan to teach you how to rope and ride."

Then his son did something so unexpected, it shot straight to his heart. Chance wrapped his arms around Austin, gave him a hug and said, "I'm glad you're my dad."

Austin swallowed around the lump in his throat. If someone would have told him a year ago that he would feel so much love for a child he'd just met, he would've called them crazy. "I'm glad you're my boy, too."

Chance climbed off the couch and faced them both. "Can we go to the barn and see my pony now?"

Georgie frowned. "What makes you think you have a pony?"

"Because if Santa can bring me my dad, he can bring me a horse."

Both Georgie and Austin laughed, sending Lila and George back into the room. "Everything settled?" Lila asked.

Chance pointed at Austin. "He's my daddy and he's going to teach me how to rope."

"Great," George groused. "Now you can traipse around the country chasing cows and women."

Lila elbowed her husband in the side. "Hush, George Romero. He can be anything he wants to be."

"I want to be a cowboy," Chance proclaimed. "And I want to see my horse."

Georgie pushed to her feet. "All right. Go get dressed and we'll go to the barn."

Chance hurried to the opening to the hall and paused to face them again. "Are you guys going to get married?"

"How would you feel about that if we do?" Georgie asked.

He shrugged. "Would we live here?"

Austin determined he should field this question. "Actually, I have a big house not far from here, with a barn and a room reserved just for you."

"Cool," he said. "Mama, you should marry my dad."

She smiled. "Then I guess it's official. We'll get married."

Seemingly satisfied, Chance took off and Austin grabbed the opportunity to take Georgie into his arms. "You heard our son. Let's get married."

"When do you propose we do this?" she asked.

"The sooner, the better. In fact, I'm thinking a New Year's Eve wedding would be good."

"That's less than a week away," Lila interjected. "We can't plan a wedding in a week."

"I don't need a fancy wedding, Mother," Georgie said. "Just family and friends and my dad to walk me down the aisle."

George stepped forward, looking less cranky than usual. "You can count on me to do that, princess."

"That's great, if we can actually find an aisle," Lila added. "Six days won't be enough time, not to mention it's a holiday."

A remedy to the time crunch entered Austin's mind. "We can have the ceremony at the ranch's main house. It's big enough to hold everyone, and I happen to know a woman who'd be glad to arrange everything, and she'll do it in record time."

"Do you mean Jenny?" Georgie asked.

"The one and only. If for some reason she can't get it done, then we'll just take a trip to the courthouse on Friday."

Lila looked mortified. "You can't marry for the first time at the courthouse."

"We did," George said. "And we're still married."

Lila scowled at him. "Don't press your luck, George Romero, if you really think you're going to force our daughter to marry in a county building."

Chance ran back into the room as fast as his boots would allow. "I'm ready to go."

Georgie slipped his hand into hers. "Then let's go."

To add to the joy of the day, Chance took Austin's hand and together they walked to the barn. They didn't talk about weddings, only the wonder of a boy's first horse, and plans for their future together. Austin executed his first duty as a father by helping Chance saddle up the pony, and keeping a watchful eye as his son rode the pen like a pro.

He draped his arm over Georgie's shoulder and pulled her close. "You've done a great job raising him, darlin'."

"It was easy. He's a great kid."

"You went to school and took care of him all by

yourself. There had to be some hard times, and I'm sorry for that."

She pressed a kiss on his cheek. "The hard times are behind us. I love you, Austin Calloway."

"Let the good times begin, and I love you, too, Georgia May Romero."

"Are you serious about the wedding in a week?" she asked.

"Yep, I am. I think it's a good way to end the old year and welcome in the new."

"If we can get it together."

He kissed her in earnest then gave her a smile. "I'd bet my last buck that Jenny will find a way to pull it off."

Georgie couldn't believe Jenny had pulled it off. The downstairs parlor was fraught with floral arrangements, the food was ready for consumption by the guests and the mint juleps were chilling in the fridge. She was dressed in a short satin gown with a lace cutout in the back and a pair of three-inch matching heels that Paris had insisted Georgie wear because she couldn't. The last she'd heard, the groom was pacing nervously throughout the family homestead and her parents' appearance hadn't started another uncivil war. Everything seemed to be going as planned. Almost everything. The officiate was still missing.

Five minutes ago, Maria had announced that the

local justice of the peace, Bucky Cheevers, had been detained by another duty for another hour. Georgie worried that if his reputation rang true, he might be holed up with a woman. That was okay, as long as he finally showed up, which he promised he would. She could think of far worse things to stall a wedding.

"My water broke."

She hadn't considered that one. Georgie turned to Paris, now standing in the doorway wearing a bathrobe, not her bridesmaid's dress. "Are you sure?"

She shuffled over to the bed and perched on the edge of the mattress. "Yes, I'm very sure. I started having some twinges yesterday afternoon, and now they're... Oh, lord, I think this baby is going to come very soon."

Georgie rushed over to her and said, "Lie down." She then hurried to the top of the stairs to sound the alarm. "Dallas, get up here now. Someone call 911 for Paris."

She returned to Paris and sat by her side. "Just take some deep breaths and try to relax, although that won't be easy under the circumstance."

Paris gave her an apologetic look. "I'm so sorry, Georgie. I'm ruining your wedding."

Georgie took her hand. "You don't need to apologize. Besides, Bucky isn't even here yet. We can always wait a couple of days. Your baby can't."

The sound of pounding footsteps echoed through

the corridor, followed by Dallas bursting into the room. "What's wrong?"

Paris lifted her head from the pillow. "We're going to have a baby."

He looked somewhat relieved. "I know that."

"Today," Paris added.

Now Dallas looked panicked as he rounded the bed and claimed a spot next to his wife. "Can you hold off?"

Paris grimaced and laid her hand on her belly. "I'm trying, honey, but maybe you should propose that to your son or daughter."

Maria rushed in with Jenny trailing behind her. "The paramedics are on their way. They should be here in five minutes."

"Five minutes I can do..." Paris sucked in a ragged breath. "I think."

"Should I boil some water just in case?" Jenny asked.

"Sure," Maria answered. "And while you're in the kitchen, have a drink. Or two."

Georgie peered behind the mothers, half expecting to see her future husband. "Where's Austin?"

"He's downstairs with Chance," Maria said.

"I told him it was bad luck to see the bride before the wedding," Jenny added. "If there's going to be a wedding. What am I going to do with all that food?"

"We're going to eat it," Maria muttered. "Now is not the time to worry about the nuptials or the catering. Austin and Georgie can still get married, even if we have to hold it at midnight after Paris delivers."

From the pain crossing Paris's face, Georgie doubted the next Calloway grandchild would wait that long.

Sitting in a hospital waiting room for five hours was not a part of Austin's plan. But here he was, dressed in suit and tie, with his almost-bride by his side and his son leaning against his shoulder, fast asleep. Jenny played games on her cell phone across from them while Maria focused on an Old West rerun playing on the TV suspended from the ceiling in the corner. George kept nodding off and, when he snored, Lila periodically shook him awake. Instead of a wedding, they'd inadvertently created a scene straight out of a weird reality show.

Austin had a good mind to go after Bucky Cheevers. If the jerk would have showed up on time, the wedding would already be over. Instead, they were clock-watching and coming to attention every time the Labor and Delivery door opened.

"What a way to ring in the New Year," he whispered to avoid disturbing Chance, who'd just settled down.

"We still have twenty minutes before the New Year is here," Georgie whispered back. "I'm surprised the baby is taking this long. I thought for sure Paris would have delivered in the ambulance."

That would've saved them this waiting game.

As good luck would have it, two minutes later, Dallas came through the door, holding a blue bundle in his arm. "I'd like you to introduce you to Lucas James Calloway."

Everyone scurried out of their seats to catch a glimpse of the newest member of the Calloway family. Everyone but Austin. He didn't believe for a minute that his own son would care to be disturbed from sleep to meet his cousin. But as bad luck would have it, Chance stirred anyway, rubbed his eyes and asked, "Are we gettin' married now?"

"Not yet, bud," Austin told him. "That probably won't happen until tomorrow."

"Come see little Lucas, Chance," Georgie said. "He reminds me of you when you were born."

Chance looked like he'd rather eat dirt, although he grudgingly climbed off the couch to answer his mother's summons. Austin followed him over to Maria who was now holding the baby. Chance took a quick peek then frowned. "He's all wrinkly and his hair is sticking up."

Georgie smiled. "That's what babies look like when they're first born."

"Okay." Obviously disinterested, Chance returned to the couch, stretched out on his back and closed his eyes.

Georgie slid her arm around Austin's waist and regarded Dallas. "Is Paris okay?"

"She's not as tired as I thought she'd be," he said. "She is relieved it's over."

Jenny took the baby from Maria without asking. "Oh my. He looks just like Worth did when he was a baby, minus the blond hair."

Austin leaned over to verify that. As far as he was concerned, the kid looked like every other kid at that stage. And he wasn't as good-looking as *his* kid. "I think he looks more like Grandpa Calloway before he got his dentures."

Georgie pinched his side. "Stop it."

"I'm sorry we blew the wedding," Dallas said.

So was Austin. "We'll figure something out in the next day or so."

Jenny handed the baby to Dallas and uttered, "I'll be right back," then pushed out the door and disappeared into the lobby.

"I better get this guy back to his mother," Dallas said. "She's going to think we left without her. She's a little disappointed he didn't arrive after the New Year so he could be the first one born."

"When can we see Paris?" Georgie asked.

Dallas glanced at the clock. "I'll check, but she should be ready for guests in a few minutes."

After Dallas walked out of the room, Jenny returned with a tall man in tow. "Georgie, Austin, this is Chaplain Griggs. He'll be glad to perform the wedding ceremony so you won't have to wait."

Austin exchanged a look with Georgie. "Do you

really want to get married in a hospital waiting room?"

Georgie shook her head. "No, but I wouldn't mind getting married in Paris's hospital room, if she's up to it. That way we can all be together as planned."

"I can do that," the chaplain said. "As long as medical personnel clear it."

"And Paris," Maria added. "She might not be up to it."

Lila stepped forward. "Georgie, honey, this isn't much better than the courthouse."

Georgie patted Lila's cheek. "It's okay, Mom. It's unique, like all of us."

"I'll drink to that," George said. "Too bad I don't have a drink handy."

"Before we go any further," the chaplain began, "I need to find out if we're cleared to continue. I'll let you know in a few minutes."

After the clergyman left, Austin turned to Georgie to find out if she was in fact serious. "If you're sure about this, I have the license."

"I'm very sure, but I don't have a bouquet."

Jenny crossed the room to an end table, yanked the fake flowers from a crystal vase and handed them to Georgie. "Here you go. It's not perfect, but it should do. Hopefully they won't send you a bill."

Maria pulled her cell from the pocket of her plain blue dress. "I'll call the other boys, just in case."

Austin saw several problems with that. "Don't

bother, Mom. Before we left the house, they told me they were going to have a few beers, and I don't see any one of them being a designated driver. Besides, if we're going to get this show on the road, we have ten minutes before midnight arrives. I'd like to stick to at least one of our original plans to be married before the New Year."

"You could also use the chapel, sugar," Jenny said. "If the room doesn't work out."

"It's going to work out fine." All eyes turned to the chaplain as he continued. "I have been instructed that we need to have a quick ceremony out of respect to the new mother. Now if you're ready, follow me."

Lila went over and nudged Chance. "Time for a wedding, baby boy."

Chance hopped off the couch and grinned. "About time."

Austin couldn't agree more.

As they wandered down the sterile corridor, their son between them, Austin took Georgie's hand and gave it a squeeze. When he imagined what they must look like to strangers, a bevy of guests dressed in their finest, he couldn't help but chuckle.

They arrived at Paris's room a few moments later, where George offered his arm to Georgie. "Son, I've waited a long time to give my daughter away, and even though we don't have an aisle, I'd like to at least walk her into the room."

He didn't dare argue with a man who had a grip on his future bride. "Not a problem, sir."

"Should I sing?" Jenny asked.

"Good heavens, no," Maria answered. "You'll wake every baby on the floor and every dog in the county."

They pushed through the door where the chaplain immediately claimed a spot near the window.

Paris was sitting up in the bed, holding the baby close, Dallas at her side. "I'm tickled pink you're doing this, you two," she said. "Just excuse my not-very-chic attire."

Georgie kissed her dad's cheek, walked over to Paris and gave her a hug. "I couldn't have a wedding without my maid of honor standing up for me. And don't worry about standing."

The chaplain cleared his throat. "Shall we begin?"

Austin checked the black clock on the wall. They had all of four minutes to get this done. "You bet."

He guided Georgie and Chance to the officiate, who started off by saying, "At times the best moments in life come in the face of a miracle. And it appears it took a miracle for you both to get to this point."

"Amen," George said from behind them, drawing more laughter.

"Would you like traditional vows, or do you plan to say your own?" the chaplain asked.

"Our own," Georgie replied before Austin could even think.

She turned to face him and smiled. "Austin, we've both traveled differing paths, but all my roads led to you. I feel blessed to have you as my husband, and the father of our child, for the rest of our life."

Austin could only come up with a few short and simple words to say. "Georgie, it's always been you. It will always be only you. Thank you for giving me our son, and the opportunity to make up for lost moments. I promise I will stay this time, forever. I love you."

She swiped at her eyes. "I love you, too."

"Do we have rings?" the chaplain asked.

"I do." Dallas stood, fished the bands from his pocket, then passed them off to Maria who handed them to the chaplain.

They slid the rings onto each other's fingers, sealing the deal, and Austin happily obliged the directive to kiss the bride. He responded to the tug on his hand with a grin aimed at his boy. "Are we married now?" Chance asked.

Austin scooped his son up into his arms. "Yeah, bud, we are. Now let's go home and get you to bed."

"To our home," Jenny said. "We still have all that food and drink."

George clasped Lila's hand. "I'm more than ready for that drink."

"I'm ready for sleep," Paris said. "Congratulations to both of you. We'll celebrate large when we come home."

After the marriage license was signed, and Austin paid the man who married them with a minute to spare, everyone said their goodbyes to the new mother and baby, then filed into the parking lot. Georgie settled Chance into his booster in the backseat then turned and slid her arms around Austin's waist. "Maria is going to put Chance to bed in your old room. That way, we can have our honeymoon at your house."

"Our house," he amended. "I believe we should forego the food and drink, unless you're hungry."

"Only for your attention," she said as she pinched his butt.

He faked a flinch. "You've got it. And you've got me from now on. Can you handle it?"

"I don't know. You can be pretty tough to take, but I'll manage." She studied his eyes, her expression surprisingly sober. "We have a lot of catching up to do, Austin, and it's going to take a lot of adjustments to our lives, raising Chance together."

He cupped her pretty face in his palms and brushed a kiss across her lips. "We can make it through anything together, sweetheart. Just look how far we've come to get to this point."

"And look at what we've got."

When they turned their attention to their sleeping son, a host of emotions ran through Austin. Awe.

Amazement. The fierce need to protect him. Above all, an unexpected, abiding love.

Yeah, he'd made more than a few mistakes, failed at a few endeavors, feared he might continue that pattern. But with his cherished Georgie by his side, Austin no longer worried if he would falter because he knew he would. And that was okay. For the first time in his life, he knew what it took to be a deserving husband and father, a real man, and it had nothing to do with how much money he made, or how many championships he'd won. It had everything to do with opening himself to love, and that much he had done. And damn if it didn't feel good.

A year ago, if anyone would've told him he'd be married and have a kid, he would've called them crazy. But now, he called himself blessed.

* * * * *

Don't miss the first story in TEXAS EXTREME:
Six rich and sexy cowboy brothers live—
and love—to the extreme!

THE RANCHER'S MARRIAGE PACT

And pick up these other flirty, feisty reads
from Kristi Gold!

THE RETURN OF THE SHEIKH
ONE NIGHT WITH THE SHEIKH
THE SHEIKH'S SON
ONE HOT DESERT NIGHT
THE SHEIKH'S SECRET HEIR

All available now from Harlequin Desire!

If you're on Twitter, tell us what you think of
Harlequin Desire! #harlequindesire

#2497 THE HEIR'S UNEXPECTED BABY

Billionaires and Babies • by Jules Bennett

A billionaire investigator and his assistant vow to bring down a crime family even as they protect an orphaned baby from the fallout—and give in to their undeniable attraction! But the secrets she's keeping may destroy all they've been working for...

#2498 TWO-WEEK TEXAS SEDUCTION

Texas Cattleman's Club: Blackmail • by Cat Schield

If Brandee doesn't seduce wealthy cowboy Shane into relinquishing his claim to her ranch, she will lose everything. So she makes a wager with him—winner take all. But victory in this game of temptation may mean losing her heart...

#2499 FROM ENEMIES TO EXPECTING

Love and Lipstick • by Kat Cantrell

Billionaire Logan needs media coverage. Marketing executive Trinity needs PR buzz. And when these opposites are caught in a lip lock, *everyone* pays attention! But this fake relationship is about to turn very real when Trinity finds out she's pregnant...

#2500 ONE NIGHT WITH THE TEXAN

The Masters of Texas • by Lauren Canan

One wild, crazy night in New Orleans will change their lives forever. He doesn't want a family. She doesn't need his accusations of entrapment. Once back in Texas, will they learn the hard way that they need each other?

#2501 THE PREGNANCY AFFAIR

Accidental Heirs • by Elizabeth Bevarly

When mafia billionaire Tate Hawthorne's dark past leads him to time in a safe house, he's confined with his sexy, secret-keeping attorney Renata Twigg. Resist her for an entire week? Impossible. But this affair may have consequences...

#2502 REINING IN THE BILLIONAIRE

by Dani Wade

Once he was only the stable hand and she broke his heart. Now he's back after earning a fortune, and he vows to make her pay. But there is more to this high-society princess—and he plans to uncover it all!

REQUEST YOUR FREE BOOKS!
2 FREE NOVELS PLUS 2 FREE GIFTS!

H HARLEQUIN®

Desire

ALWAYS POWERFUL, PASSIONATE AND PROVOCATIVE

YES! Please send me 2 FREE Harlequin® Desire novels and my 2 FREE gifts (gifts are worth about $10). After receiving them, if I don't wish to receive any more books, I can return the shipping statement marked "cancel." If I don't cancel, I will receive 6 brand-new novels every month and be billed just $4.55 per book in the U.S. or $5.24 per book in Canada. That's a savings of at least 13% off the cover price! It's quite a bargain! Shipping and handling is just 50¢ per book in the U.S. and 75¢ per book in Canada.* I understand that accepting the 2 free books and gifts places me under no obligation to buy anything. I can always return a shipment and cancel at any time. Even if I never buy another book, the two free books and gifts are mine to keep forever.

225/326 HDN GH2P

Name	(PLEASE PRINT)

Address	Apt. #

City	State/Prov.	Zip/Postal Code

Signature (if under 18, a parent or guardian must sign)

Mail to the **Reader Service:**

IN U.S.A.: P.O. Box 1867, Buffalo, NY 14240-1867
IN CANADA: P.O. Box 609, Fort Erie, Ontario L2A 5X3

Want to try two free books from another line?
Call 1-800-873-8635 or visit www.ReaderService.com.

* Terms and prices subject to change without notice. Prices do not include applicable taxes. Sales tax applicable in N.Y. Canadian residents will be charged applicable taxes. Offer not valid in Quebec. This offer is limited to one order per household. Not valid for current subscribers to Harlequin Desire books. All orders subject to credit approval. Credit or debit balances in a customer's account(s) may be offset by any other outstanding balance owed by or to the customer. Please allow 4 to 6 weeks for delivery. Offer available while quantities last.

Your Privacy—The Reader Service is committed to protecting your privacy. Our Privacy Policy is available online at www.ReaderService.com or upon request from the Reader Service.

We make a portion of our mailing list available to reputable third parties that offer products we believe may interest you. If you prefer that we not exchange your name with third parties, or if you wish to clarify or modify your communication preferences, please visit us at www.ReaderService.com/consumerchoice or write to us at Reader Service Preference Service, P.O. Box 9062, Buffalo, NY 14240-9062. Include your complete name and address.

HDI5

A billionaire investigator and his assistant vow to bring
down a crime family even as they protect an orphaned
baby from the fallout—and give in to their undeniable
attraction! But the secrets she's keeping may destroy all
they've been working for…

Read on for a sneak peek at
THE HEIR'S UNEXPECTED BABY
by Jules Bennett, part of the bestselling
BILLIONAIRES AND BABIES series!

"What are you doing here so early?"

Jack Carson brushed past Vivianna Smith and stepped
into her apartment, trying like hell not to touch her. Or
breathe in that familiar jasmine scent. Or think of how sexy
she looked in that pale pink suit.

Masochist. That's all he could chalk this up to. But he
had a mission, damn it, and he needed his assistant's help
to pull it off.

"I need you to use that charm of yours and get more
information about the O'Sheas." He turned to face her as
she closed the door.

The O'Sheas might run a polished high-society auction
house, but he knew they were no better than common
criminals. And Jack was about to bring them down in a
spectacular show of justice. His ticket was the woman who
fueled his every fantasy.

Vivianna moved around him to head down the hall to the
nursery. "I'm on your side here," she told him with a soft

smile. "Why don't you come back this evening and I'll make dinner and we can figure out our next step."

Dinner? With her and the baby? That all sounded so… domestic. He prided himself on keeping work in the office or in neutral territory. But he'd come here this morning to check on her…and he couldn't blame it all on the O'Sheas.

Damn it.

"You can come to my place and I'll have my chef prepare something." There. If Tilly was on hand, then maybe it wouldn't seem so family-like. "Any requests?" he asked.

Did her gaze just dart to his lips? She couldn't look at him with those dark eyes as if she wanted…

No. It didn't matter what she wanted, or what he wanted for that matter. Their relationship was business only.

Jack paused, soaking in the sight of her in that prim little suit, holding the baby. Definitely time to go before he forgot she actually worked for him and took what he'd wanted for months…

Don't miss
THE HEIR'S UNEXPECTED BABY
by Jules Bennett,
available February 2017 wherever
Harlequin® Desire books and ebooks are sold.

If you enjoyed this excerpt, pick up a new
***BILLIONAIRES AND BABIES** book every month!*

It's the #1 bestselling series from Harlequin® Desire—
Powerful men…wrapped around their babies' little
fingers.

www.Harlequin.com

Whatever You're Into… Passionate Reads

Looking for more passionate reads from Harlequin®?
Fear not! Harlequin® Presents, Harlequin® Desire and
Harlequin® Blaze offer you irresistible romance stories
featuring powerful heroes.

HARLEQUIN
Presents

Do you want alpha males, decadent glamour and jet-set
lifestyles? Step into the sensational, sophisticated world of
Harlequin® Presents, where sinfully tempting heroes ignite a
fierce and wickedly irresistible passion!

HARLEQUIN
Desire

Harlequin® Desire novels are powerful, passionate and
provocative contemporary romances set against a backdrop of
wealth, privilege and sweeping family saga. Alpha heroes with
a soft side meet strong-willed but vulnerable heroines amid a
dramatic world of divided loyalties, high-stakes conflict and
intense emotion.

HARLEQUIN
Blaze

Harlequin® Blaze stories sizzle with strong heroines and
irresistible heroes playing the game of modern love and lust.
They're fun, sexy and always steamy.

Be sure to check out our full selection of books
within each series every month!

www.Harlequin.com

HPASSION2016

Turn your love of reading into rewards you'll love with

Harlequin My Rewards

**Join for FREE today at
www.HarlequinMyRewards.com**

Earn **FREE BOOKS** of your choice.

Experience **EXCLUSIVE OFFERS** and contests.

Enjoy **BOOK RECOMMENDATIONS**
selected just for you.

PLUS! Sign up now
and get **500** points
right away!

Earn
FREE
REWARDS
Join
Today!
HarlequinMyRewards.com

MYRI6R

Love the Harlequin book you just read?

Your opinion matters.

Review this book on your favorite book site, review site, blog or your own social media properties and share your opinion with other readers!